27

A Tangled Web

by John McArdle

To Martin

Best Wishes

John McArdle

Published by JJ Moffs Independent Book Publisher 2019

JJ Moffs Independent Book Publisher Ltd
Grove House Farm, Grovewood Road,
Misterton, Nottinghamshire DN10 4EF

ISBN 978-1-9165042-4-0

Printed and bound in Great Britain by Clays Ltd, Elcograf S.p.A
Typeset and cover design by Anna Richards

I dedicate this book to my wife Gillian, my life partner and source of support in all that I do. I also want to thank her for accepting that this story is not autobiographical!

Also by John McArdle

The Elephant and the Wasp

Chapter 1

If only we could recognise when we have reached a fork in the road of life. If only we could know the consequences of turning right or left... good or bad. If we could go back in time, what would we change?

Tony Needham looked down at his desk from his executive swivelling leather chair and fixed his gaze on the small wooden block placed centrally at the rear of the rich green leatherette top. On both sides, in impressive brass lettering, it announced 'Anthony Needham, Branch Manager'. It was 7.15 am, and it had been his practice for the six years or so since his promotion to spend a few seconds every morning staring at the plaque. It was the plaque that showed his rise through the ranks of The North Yorkshire Building Society and his elevation on a ladder he had started to climb upon leaving school 20 years ago. This was now the time to reconstruct an accurate recollection of his life, his personality, and to look for those choices that everyone faces. Which fork in the road do we follow? What were we taught about right and wrong, good and bad, or black and white? It often is the tiny moment, or the seemingly unimportant decision we make, that colours the rest of our lives.

He was 36 now, and in his reflective mood he remembered that at school he had been bright, but easily distracted and often bored. His examination results were disappointing and served as a wakeup call for him. Upon leaving school, he had undertaken a number of jobs including working in a department store and for a short time as a car salesman before he applied for the post of trainee finance clerk with the society. His climb from that point had been sharper than he expected, leading to the title on the plaque. He smiled to himself when he remembered his time as a car salesman. He found it easy to charm the customers, especially the older women who tended to look on him as the kind of son they would like to have, or maybe a toy-boy about whom they fantasised. He was good with people.

He had been happy enough in his previous jobs, but he knew he could do better for himself. He could have stayed on at school and done his A Levels, but he liked the idea of earning money, especially when extra was available by way of bonus. He soon discovered that money was not the only driving force for him, as he was ambitious to have a career that brought respect and the possibility of position within the circles he wanted to move. An early school report had labelled him as sometimes too ambitious for his own good. Maybe he should have paid more attention to that.

When interviewed at the society, he found that his time as a salesman had stood him in good stead; he had a natural charm about him and a salesman's ability to find out what people were looking for. He was just over six feet tall, slim, and had a full head of thick dark brown hair, which he knew made him a physically attractive proposition to most people. He had learned whilst selling cars that people had a natural leaning towards attractive sales staff, and although he was no David Beckham, he knew he was above average. Add to that his easy charm, winning smile, and quiet confidence, and he presented as a good all-round package to customers and employers alike. At the interview, he kept telling himself to stay calm and to sound confident, but not cocky, assured but not insufferable.

He was pleased, yet not surprised, to open the mail a few days later and find that he had beaten off the opposition of eight or nine others and had secured the job. He was ambitious, as the school report had correctly identified, and interested in learning quickly. Here was a stage to show his drive and intelligence. Staged raises and minor promotions followed as he moved from branch to branch before being offered the post of assistant manager at the Harrogate branch, where he settled into the job and a town that he liked. He was happy enough with the position, but on the 22nd of May, just before his 30th birthday, the branch was thrown into disarray.

Colin Marshall had been the branch manager for 15 years and was an amiable and very capable boss who had shown him the ropes. He had also helped him settle into the town by inviting him along to dinners and introducing him to local solicitors and estate agents. In fact, on the 20th May, Colin had taken Tony to a law society dinner as guests of Appleton, Townsend and Palmer, a local firm of solicitors, and they had both probably eaten and drunk a little too much. Colin was in his late fifties, thinning hair, three stone overweight, and with a liking for cigars, which he indulged on the night. He was always very good company and seemed to know everybody at that dinner and indeed most places they went. It seemed that most people wanted to buy him a drink, and Colin rarely said no to their generosity.

As they said goodbye in separate taxis that night, Colin looked a little red in the face as he was driven back to his family home just outside of Leeds. Two days later in the office, Colin's red pallor had changed to a faint grey, and although he insisted he was fine, Tony suggested he take the day off.

'Looks like you should have said no to that last bottle of red on Saturday night, Colin,' Tony whispered as he went past him.

'I can drink you under the table anytime, Needers,' was the reply with a laugh.

As Tony walked away, he turned to smile back and noticed that Colin had a row of beads of sweat just above his eyebrows and his smile had quickly disappeared from his face.

Two hours into the day Colin got up from his seat, turned to collect his tea from the table behind him, and fell to the ground like a felled tree. The noise stopped all activity in the branch, including the serving of customers at the glass, protected tills, and the financial advisor's desk. It was one of those noises that you knew instinctively was the background to real trouble and not something that would end in a jolly apology and a funny anecdote. Tony was checking the mortgage arrears register when he heard the noise, and he turned, silently but quickly, before mouthing to nobody in particular, *'What the hell was that?'*

The paramedics said that Colin was dead as he hit the floor. They said it was a massive heart attack that must have been coming for some time, and there was nothing they could do to revive him, despite being there 14 minutes after the three nines call. There were six other members of staff apart from Tony, and they were all in tears as they tried to assimilate the pictures in their heads and the fact that their much-loved boss was dead and worse still had died right in front of them. Tony found himself to be calm and unflustered, despite his own sorrow and shock. He rose to the challenge of being temporary captain and made all necessary calls, closed the branch, and soothed his colleagues. It was only when he was at home, sitting in his armchair, sipping a sedating whisky that the selfish thought of promotion filtered into his thoughts. At first, he dismissed it as tasteless and ungrateful for the tuition, but he was unable to repel it for long. An unpleasant, selfish thought had been released, and the genie would not go back into the bottle. He would be the youngest manager in the group, but surely he was the obvious choice as he knew the systems so well, knew the staff and their abilities as well as being the local man known by all the customers. Eventually, the moral conflict of the confused emotions caused his eyelids to feel heavy before he drifted off into a fitful but deep sleep.

Being a man down over the next few weeks brought a great deal of pressure, especially as a second casualty, Irene, quickly followed Colin's demise. She was Colin's PA, and due to the stress of the fatal event she handed in a three-week sick note. Tony had often thought that the thirty-something Irene was a little more than a PA to Colin. He had once gone into Colin's room to find Irene sitting at the front of his desk looking down at Colin sitting in his chair, a little too close for professional comfort. His suspicions increased when the sound of the door caused Irene to leap from the semi-sitting position and Colin to swivel in his chair so quickly that his spectacles nearly flew off.

'Oh it's you, Needers, nearly scared me to death. Ever heard of knocking?' spluttered Colin, almost confirming the position. Think yourself lucky I wasn't your wife, was Tony's immediate, unspoken thought but they never spoke of it then or ever.

Anyway, the position at work now was burdensome as not only were they shorthanded, but the footfall into the office was hugely increased as well-meaning customers and professional contacts came in to find out what had happened, and to offer their sympathy. The most significant visit was from Andrew Maxwell, the regional manager, who spent an hour with Tony and during it, made him acting manager and offered him an assistant. Tony's smart card was to suggest the promotion of Melanie Forrester from cashier to that role and to take a junior as her replacement. This promotion made it more difficult for the society to bring in a new manager from outside, as it would make their little team a little top heavy. The strategy worked, as six weeks later his appointment was made formal, which lead to the brass nameplate he enjoyed so much. Not for the first or last time, Tony had been able to manipulate the situation to his advantage.

Reflection can be both enjoyable and painful. Gently swaying in his chair, he remembered the day his parents paid a visit when he welcomed them into his new office. His mother, never far from tears, shed a few more upon entering, but his father was his usual cold, semi-aggressive self as he ambled around the room looking at the pictures and the certificates without saying a word. Tony's father was a short, stocky man who had spent most of his life in a local food-processing factory and lived a life typical of a manual worker. He left the house at the same time every day, returned at the same time every evening tired from a day of physical toil, which made him irritable and sensitive. Tony had a complicated relationship with him and saw his Dad develop a chip on his shoulder as he realised his son was more intelligent than him. He would be prepared for his father's retaliation in advance of perceived patronage and regular barbed comments such as, 'Anybody spill tea on you today, boy?' or, 'Been lifting any heavy files? Better have a lie-down.' The pain for Tony was that he did not feel like that at all. Even though he was earning more than his father, he admired his Dad and had always seen him as the head of the family and someone above all others he wanted to impress. It was maybe for that reason that Tony always focused on the plaque because that day, the day of his parents visit, his father had arrived at the desk after wandering around the room and picked up the wooden nameplate without changing expression. He held it for a few seconds, silently but intently staring at the lettering spelling out his son's name, before putting it down, looking up at his son and winking. The wink was followed by three nods of approval, which filled Tony's heart with such pride that he thought the sound of the beating coming out of his chest might be audible in the street. There it was in that moment, the long-awaited sign of approval and admiration from his father.

Tony wondered if that was the best day of his life. If it was not, he was struggling to think of a better one. The promotion, salary increase, and the improved prospects, on top of his father's reaction, had created a new and exciting chapter for him. He looked forward to every new day and the chance to go into the office as the boss; to refer to himself as manager in telephone calls, and to even think that he might be taking Andrew Maxwell's post as regional manager in a few years. Who knew where it might end? Possibly as a director in his mid-forties, with a house and car to match?

As he sat reflecting on all of this, he looked back up at the clock, now showing 7.22 am, and took one final look at his name on the desk before asking himself again. When did all of this go wrong, and when did I become a thief?

Chapter 2

Do you become a thief with a single thought or act, or do you slide gently into dishonesty without noticing your feet losing grip on a law-abiding pathway? Is the capacity for risk and possible self-destruction endless?

He could remember where the dark road started, and it was so innocent, even noble, if you thought about it long enough. The new junior cashier, Maureen Bradley, had been working for about six months and was doing very well. She was a petite, blonde haired girl with an unfortunate habit of sitting round-shouldered and looking upwards from an almost crouching position on the till, giving the impression of her being subservient when looking at customers. Tony had brought this to her attention, and she was trying her best to sit upright and look confident.

She had been working, almost unsupervised, at her station for five weeks and had improved her posture and confidence level, as well as being popular within the team. On this particular Friday night, she had knocked at Tony's door, stumbled in, and burst into uncontrollable tears. She managed to blurt out that at lunchtime she had taken a cash payment from a customer of £300 and had correctly entered it into the customer's passbook as well as recording it as a daily receipt. She had, however, placed the cash in an envelope as the vault was not open, and the two key holders were out at lunch. When she returned from lunch, she had completely forgotten about it. The day's banking had now been done, and the cash was still in her desk. Maureen had been told in her training that all cash had to be banked at the end of the day or balanced with the cash float retained by the society. There would now be a day discrepancy and, as it was cash, a disciplinary investigation. Tony realised there was nothing dishonest and when she confirmed that nobody knew about it, he said he had a solution. He would register the discrepancy as a recording error, as he was able to do by entering the manager's code into the system. He would then take the money home with him and record it as an entry on Monday to put things right. No audit trail would check the customer's passbook to notice the different dates and everything would be in order. Maureen was told that this was the first and only time he would do this, and he expected a big improvement. She was, of course, delighted and promised unwavering devotion for this unexpected reprieve. Truth to tell, Tony also realised that the incident, if reported, would reflect badly on him since Maureen was his choice on interview as well as his idea of everyone moving up when Colin had died. It was a bit of a risk, but better than having a black mark against his branch. He had taken the cash home and looked after it, like a bird watching her eggs, until Monday when it was banked and the error erased.

Was it that incident that had implanted a dark seed in his mind of systems and the exploitation of them? He started to see loopholes everywhere, and although most had safeguards when a hypothetical theft or fraud was followed through in his mind, not all did. He began an obsession with the security side of the business and at one point speculated on writing a paper on it and offering advice to his employers to advance his career. He very nearly mentioned it when Andrew Maxwell popped in for a progress report on the branch but decided he needed to think about it a little more before any discussion. If he was going to have that discussion, then he should prove his theory that the theft or fraud can be done easily and recommend the failsafe cure for the fault in the system. The thought of this set his pulse racing as a surge of adrenalin ran through his body, and his excitement levels soared. He had to be careful, as failure in his chosen task might have the opposite effect and make him look foolish, or worse, make him look dishonest, which he knew he was not. There were a number of potential starting points, but he settled on the cash payments counted at the tills. Some of the local trades' people used the society as a sort of bank. Instead of paying all of their receipts into a bank current account, they paid money into their building society account, as they were paid interest on the balance they had.

One such customer was Fiona Cummings who was a local farmer he knew well. She was in her mid-fifties and looked like a farmer in that her multi coloured hair was always pointing in all directions. Her face had never seen cosmetics but had a healthy outdoor complexion, and her clothes were either green or brown, finished off with boots or wellingtons. Fiona had opened a farm shop on her premises and sold eggs, bacon, bread, preserves, and any other produce she could source. The addition of the coffee shop had increased her takings enormously, but her systems were chaotic. She tended to bluster into the branch with a bag full of cash and then scramble through her handbag to find her passbooks. To add to the confusion, she had four accounts that offered different rates of interest as they had different conditions attached to them. The sight of Fiona coming into the branch led to the staff looking to the ground, answering a phantom telephone call, or anything to try and have her use another till before she settled at one and the inevitable 20-minute transaction. Money was counted out, and a figure confirmed for Fiona to approve and sign the appropriate form which was often redone as she discovered another £100 or so in her handbag. There was no check on the till and no way of knowing that the money taken corresponded with the amount recorded. This would be the first experiment. A line was created and would soon be crossed.

Tony often filled in on the tills if they were short staffed and knowing Fiona was due in on this particular Friday he would make sure he was there to serve her. He wrote a note on his computer at home, which he knew would have the time and date of the typing, to say that he was going to test the system for vulnerability, and there was no better start than a vulnerable customer. The note would protect him if something went wrong.

Fiona duly turned up when two tills were in use, and Tony was at one of them. Theresa Mullin, the most experienced clerk, was at the other till and, upon seeing

Fiona, put her head down and started writing furiously. Tony beckoned Fiona forward.

'Hello, Fiona, I haven't seen you for ages; how is business for you?'

'Oh, the usual. Too many people and not enough hands to help,' she said laughing. She tipped out her bundle of notes and coins and then started the search for the passbooks.

'I'll count it first, and then you can tell me where it's going.'

'Oh yes please, I can never find these bloody books.' Tony separated the notes into twenties, tens, and fives, and with the aid of the counting machine came up with a total of £3,865. The coins total was £486.25.

'Okay, Fiona, we have £3,665 in notes and £436.25 in coins, where do you want it to go?'

'Oh put half of it in this one and the other half in that,' she replied handing over two books whilst sorting out her enormous handbag and dropping papers on the floor. Tony duly complied with the request and then entered the amount on the daily sheet entry to correspond with the passbook. Fiona chatted about her family for a few minutes and then left as breezily as she had arrived without any knowledge that she had just been deprived of £250 and no way of ever knowing. Tony removed £250 in notes under cover of a file and when back in his office placed the notes in an envelope which he marked Property of Fiona Cummings - security experiment 1. He then placed the envelope in his bottom left-hand side drawer in his desk and locked it.

There was a surge of an emotion he had never quite felt before. It was like a combination of sexual energy and menacing fear. His pulse rate had quickened to the extent that he could feel his temples pulsating; a trickle of sweat inched its way from his armpit to nestle in his shirt, and moisture dried inside his mouth. This was it; there was no going back, and he knew he had crossed a line. As so often in life, he knew then what he had done, but the persuasive skills we all possess started to work as he compiled the arguments of justification and righteousness. He was, after all, looking out for the interests of his employer and ultimately safeguarding the valued customers of the building society. Yes, that was it, that was what he was doing, and if a small promotion came his way, well that was a by-product of his efforts.

When he arrived at the branch the next day, he half expected a police car to be outside or a raging Fiona with a handful of receipts asking what had happened to her money. Instead, there was just the normal sleepy start to another standard day. Theresa Mullin knocked on his door and popped her head in.

'Can I have a word, Tony?'

Oh my God, did she see something? Could she tell he was different? Had her experience of all the years at the branch caused her to smell a dubious act?

'Yes, of course, Theresa, have a seat.' She sat down looking a little flustered and pulled out of her handbag a number of bank statements.

'It's about my Aunty Dorothy, Tony. She is well into

her eighties, and we think she is going a bit doolally. I
shouldn't say that because she is a lovely lady, but she is
getting forgetful, and it may be dementia setting in. She is
normally okay, but my sister and I found about £500 lying
in a drawer, and she couldn't remember where it came
from. She has all these accounts from when Uncle Billy
was alive, and we think they need sorting out.'

Tony was just relieved that the discussion was not about
him, and he had not yet fully engaged with the conversation.
Playing for time and composure he asked,

'Are you sure she has the capacity to make decisions?'

'Oh yes, most of the time she is absolutely fine, and she
can tell you, word for word, a conversation she had fifty
years ago. She just forgets she put the cooker on for dinner
or forgets what she has gone into a room for. Mind you, I
do that myself.'

Tony was now relaxed and fully engaged in the potential
question.

'So what is it you want to do, Theresa?'

Theresa smiled and placed the statements on Tony's desk.

'I am a bit too close to do it myself, but I wondered if
you would pop out and see her and talk to her about the
accounts we have, and we can arrange to close all of these
and keep them under our roof. Some of these accounts
pay no interest, and she has about £120,000 in the ones we
have found.'

'Wow, Uncle Billy was a bit of a saver, was he?'

'Not really, they lived in the same house all of their
married lives, and she still does. Also, they never spent
anything on themselves, but were always kind to my sister

and me. Dorothy is my Mum's sister.'

'Okay, Theresa, set up a meeting next week and I will pop out to see her. I am sure we can do better than these accounts,' he said flicking through the statements. As Theresa left, he took out the key from his top pocket and opened his desk drawer to look at the envelope containing Fiona's money and the reassuring phrase he had placed on it demonstrating that it was an experiment, and that he was treating the contents as Fiona's property. The trouble was that the envelope was still there three weeks later, and he had no explanation why. Also, he had opened the door to greater opportunity where people would present themselves as sheep before a wolf.

Chapter 3

On the evening following the chat with Theresa, Tony had taken the short drive to his home on the outskirts of Harrogate. He could not afford to live in the town but had bought a fairly large four bedroomed house on a new estate, which was comfortably the best property anyone in his extended family owned. He had borrowed the maximum allowance on a mortgage from his employers at the preferential staff rate, and as it was his fifth move in seven years, he had built up a nice amount of equity in the property.

His house had two garages, which housed his two-year-old Nissan and his wife's small Skoda. When Jemma became pregnant with Anna, a little over nine years ago, he had married her even though that was a little old fashioned, but so was he. Jemma was one in a long line of girlfriends, although she was a cut above most of the others he had been out with. She was blonde, slim, and attractive in a girl next door sort of way, but she was also funny and bright. If he was honest with himself, he was flattered that a middle-class girl like her was attracted to a working-class product like him. Jemma's parents lived in a detached house just outside of Leeds and had always been kind and welcoming to him. He felt he struggled to compete with Jemma's Dad, who was a very successful surveyor, and maybe his inferiority complex was a reason for the marriage proposal on the news of the pregnancy. Jemma herself had taken the full maternity leave from her job as a travel agent and now worked part-time. Toby was born two years after his sister to complete their little family.

Driving up to his house he took a moment to look closely at it and saw that Jemma had planted some shrubs on the edge of the entrance to the front door. She had a real eye for this sort of thing in making the garden look mature and perfectly matched. She applied the same touch of class inside, as the furnishings and decor were stylish and expensive looking, even when bought cheaply. Jemma's Dad had been very generous with the wedding present and gifts since then, which Tony appreciated but would love to be able to emulate from his own efforts. The desire to climb the ladder of success and enjoy the trappings that came with it was building inside him, especially rubbing shoulders with those who had already achieved it. Desire can be a dangerous beast, and the exposure to lavish living can be either positive or negative: positive if it sharpens the work ethic, but negative if it induces an unhealthy haste for reward. Can it turn a sheep into a wolf?

A few days after the chat in the office, Tony called upon Theresa's Aunty Dorothy who met him at the door of her bungalow with a beaming smile as she extended her right hand.

'Oh, this is so kind of you, Mr Needham; Theresa talks so highly of you, and you must be so busy. Please, come in and let me make you a cup of tea. I have made a chocolate cake just for you.'

Tony looked around the well-appointed but dated property and the photographs of her family.

'You have a lovely home, Mrs Madeley, how long have you lived here?' he asked as she prepared the tea.

'52 years this August,' she answered.

Tony made himself comfortable, drank the tea, ate the delicious cake, and worked through all of the papers she had piled on the coffee table. Whilst looking through them, he noticed an old share certificate in the name of Westminster Insurance Services, which was a company that closed about twenty years ago.

'Do you know what this relates to, Mrs Madeley?'

'Please, call me Dorothy... let me have a look... oh, I think Billy had some shares in it years ago, but I don't know what happened to them. He probably cashed them in.'

Tony made a list of all of the accounts and asked Dorothy what she spent her money on and how much access she needed to it. She had a pension and half of her deceased husband's pension, which was enough for her needs, leaving the rest of the money to accumulate. He was able to show Dorothy that without taking risks she could increase the monthly interest she would receive and think about spending that on treats for herself and her family. She enjoyed the company of someone to talk to as much as the news she was getting and clearly felt honoured that the manager had taken the time to come and see her. Tony asked if he could take the share certificate away and check it.

Back at the office, Tony checked the history of the Westminster Insurance Services Company and saw that it was taken over by a larger company 26 years ago, and then that larger company was itself taken over by the Prudential Insurance Company 10 years ago. By checking the share numbers, he was able to establish that they had been converted into Prudential shares. He got Theresa to prepare a form of authority for Dorothy to sign and wrote to the Prudential to obtain confirmation. A week or so later a letter arrived from the Prudential to inform him that the shares carried dividends, which had been unpaid due to a clerical error with Billy's address. The accumulation of the dividends, share value, and goodwill payment for the error came to a total of £18,766.64, and upon production of the death certificate of Mr Madeley, a cheque would be sent to conclude. When Tony gave the news to Theresa, she gasped and then started to cry. Through the tears, she told Tony that she had seen the certificate but thought nothing of it, as she just believed that as the company no longer existed it had no value. She was so glad she had gone to him and that he was clever enough to know what to do. Aunty Dorothy would be delighted and would surely make him another cake.

He enjoyed the praise and the achievement, but a darker thought had set seed, and as much as he tried to deny it, the seed was implanted and would grow. This was an insight into the large amount of funds held by people who neither understood them nor were careful in protecting them. More importantly, he could have engineered something here, and Dorothy would have signed anything put before her without any likely investigation. Dorothy was a little close to home with her niece working for him, but there were hundreds of accounts with elderly customers who would not miss some of their funds. A tingle of danger and excitement rippled through his body. The fork in the road was there to be seen.

Chapter 4

A glance at the clock showed him it was 7.26 am. It had taken him only eleven minutes to go through the formative years of his life; a life which had up until then been good and, above all else, honest. Why had things taken such a turn? The first major incident, following Aunty Dorothy, was easy to remember. He had accumulated seven envelopes of cash from the till trick that he had now perfected as though he was a magician using sleight of hand. The total of that cash was a little under £2,500, and his ambition was set higher. And then a Mrs Brownlee made an appointment to see him and provided the target.

She was in her mid-eighties and was partially sighted but independent. Her husband had died five years previously and had taken her enthusiasm for life with him. She was very lonely but in fear of a life of care and being a burden. This fear had been increased when her Doctor had told her that the breathlessness she had been feeling recently was lung cancer that was both incurable and inoperable. She had not asked how long she had to live but wanted to put her affairs in order and had no idea how to do it. Could Mr Needham explain what she had by way of money and arrange for a solicitor to complete a will for her. The answer was yes, and although he didn't know how, he knew that this was a big opportunity. In the hour or so they were together he established that she had funds of around £220,000 and a mortgage-free house worth twice that sum. Most interesting of all, she had no children as her husband had suffered from a childhood condition which had rendered him sterile. She had no living family apart from a nephew in Canada and a niece in London who she hardly saw. She wanted to leave them something in the memory of her sister, but the bulk of the money was going to her friend who lived next door, and the church. This set of circumstances set his mind racing as though driven by a narcotic as he plotted and planned whilst adopting his charming manner. Mrs Brownlee said she would leave all the arrangements to him and that she felt so much better having talked to him.

Two nights of tossing and turning and the plan was formulated. Integral in that plan was a solicitor he had met at a law society dinner with his former boss. He was Matthew Barker, a partner in Appleton, Townsend, and Palmer. Matthew was in his forties and had been educated at significant expense in a minor public school before embarking upon his legal career in the firm where his uncle had been senior partner. Matthew's clothes were always ill-fitting and looking in need of dry cleaning with traces of last week's lunches appearing on lapels and trousers. He was well spoken, a little portly, and most importantly, gullible.

The first phone call to Matthew was easy as the offer of new work from one professional to another is as common as it is welcome. The lawyer's predictable response was his firm would be very interested in a stream of wills and probate work and would be happy to work with him in any way he wished. After a meeting over lunch, Tony had driven Matthew to Mrs Brownlee's house for a preliminary discussion, tea, and biscuits. They agreed on an arrangement that Tony would go through all of the details later, pass them on to Matthew who would prepare the will, and Tony would arrange for it to be signed.

The plan was not foolproof but controllable. The lunch with Matthew that day had been a boozy affair, but the lawyer had not noticed that Tony did more pouring than drinking. Instead, Matthew had explained exactly how probate was obtained and how his firm dealt with the estate of the deceased. Tony's plan was that within the instructions he would deliver to Matthew there would be gifts of £30,000 each to the niece and nephew with the residue split between the church and the friendly neighbour, Mrs Carter, who was in her seventies. There was also a gift of £30,000 to a Patrick Baxter at an address in Manchester. That gift sat alongside the niece and nephew and looked like it was another random family member. Matthew had agreed that Tony would read the draft will to his client for approval and thought nothing of the contents or those benefitting from the will. He was happy to have the fee and the impending probate. All Tony had to do was set up an account for Patrick Baxter, his new alias.

He had to have a fake ID and a utility bill to be able to open an account that would receive the money when poor old Mrs Brownlee passed away. He had a few weeks which he used to great effect. His task was to obtain a passport, and he checked online what he would need: a birth certificate in the name of the applicant, and as it was a first passport, the birth certificates of both parents, and their marriage certificate. Mr and Mrs Baxter had provided the answer for him. They had opened an account two years before for their severely autistic son Patrick who was around Tony's age. Tony paid them a visit and invented potential problems they might experience in the future that he would overcome now with a change of account. That account needed a passport by way of identity, and he charmed them into applying for one. Superimposing his photograph on the original when it arrived was easy, for the purposes of being photocopied and looking real. The photocopied passport would be his route to identity evidence. Matthew had even signed five copies as true copies of the original on another boozy night when Tony had hidden his reading glasses. Now that he had the fake identity document, he rented a flat that he had spotted on the internet in a part of Manchester that was inexpensive and he knew well. He met the landlord who was happy to save an agent's fee and let the property without any further checks for a cash payment up front. His false identity was falling into place.

He now had the documents to open an account anywhere, as he also registered for electricity on the flat, which gave him his utility bill with his false name on it. The passport, the address, and the utility bill were his tickets to the creation of wealth in another name, and as long as he kept his two lives separate nobody would know. He had to choose his targets carefully and now had a template; single or widowed elderly people who knew that their end was coming but crucially did not have close family living nearby looking after them who might be suspicious of his motives. He even persuaded himself that these were victimless crimes, as the owner of the money had no use for it, and he was giving them time and comfort at the end of their lives, which was more than the distant relatives were doing.

His discussions with Matthew had shown him the opportunity in the assets of the recently deceased. There was no automatic checking of the situation and often little communication between the person dying and the people who would deal with the estate. If it were a family member who was an executor, they would often find it distressing or embarrassing to discuss matters with a loved one who was dying, and a professional executor had no knowledge of the background when receiving instructions as to a will and the distribution of the money. If he was careful, he could have a regular harvest, and nobody would be any the wiser. Harrogate to Manchester was about an hour and a half by car, so it was not too difficult to cover the journey with one of his now many outside client visits. On one of those visits, he opened two accounts at a Manchester Nat West branch with his new identity and even organised debit and credit cards.

One cold February day in the office he received a call that Mrs Brownlee had been taken into the local hospice and was not expected to last more than a week. She had asked if he could visit her if he was not too busy. He said he would go after work that day. The hospice was not a place he had visited before, and he was very surprised at how upbeat the staff members were. The atmosphere was not foreboding as he often found hospitals to be. A very pleasant receptionist took him to a brightly lit room marked with Mrs Brownlee's name, and as he entered he saw her lying in her bed staring at the wall, looking very grey in the face. He whispered her name and stepped forward to the side of the bed. She grasped his hand tightly as she told him through her tears that he had been so kind to her and that she was so sad that she had not had children. Still grasping his hand, she added that if she had been lucky enough to have a son, she would have wanted him to be like Tony. His throat tightened, and his heart sank into his shoes as he was brought into the reality of his betrayal of this lovely elderly lady who had trusted him so implicitly. She died ten days later, but by then he had worked on his pricking conscience. He moved from the position of wanting to get out of this mess and not being able to, to that the money wasn't being taken from Mrs Brownlee but from faceless relatives she hardly knew, and anyway she may have wanted him to have it. In the months that followed, he spoke often with Matthew until the day he was told that probate was through and the cheques were being sent out. On his next trip to his rented flat he felt that familiar exhilaration on the journey and then opening the flat door he saw the letter from Appleton, Townsend, and Palmer, which read;

Dear Mr Baxter,
Re: Mrs Ilene Brownlee deceased

*We are sad to report the death of our client Mrs Brownlee, who died
in February of this year. In our client's will, she bequeathed you
the sum of £30,000 and having completed the Grant of Probate
we have pleasure in enclosing our cheque for that amount. We
should be most grateful if you would acknowledge receipt of the
cheque.*
Yours Sincerely

Matthew Barker
Appleton, Townsend, and Palmer

Two days later he was looking at his online account with
a credit of £30,000 sitting in it. He transferred £25,000
into a deposit account with the bank and set up the standing
orders for rent and utilities, including his new mobile phone
registered to Patrick Baxter.

In a tense two months that followed, he wondered if an
enquiry would come from one of the relatives or the church.
No enquiry came, although Matthew did tell him that the
nephew in Canada had died a year before Mrs Brownlee,
so the church and the neighbour got a windfall of £15,000
each. Perhaps he should have been a residual beneficiary
and had a bigger slice of the cake. He had by then moved on
with other plans which were now underway. He had taken
giant steps away from the initial self-deception of carrying
out an exercise to help protect his employers from theft or

fraud. He could not bring himself to consider himself a thief, but he knew that he had left behind the normal lawful life he had been leading and there was no way back.

His relationship with Matthew was developing, and every day he was looking at customers as potential prey. A very nice old couple came in to open an account and to ask to transfer their ISAs from their bank, as they had read that The North Yorkshire Building Society paid a full 1% more in interest. They had £198,000 between them to transfer, but Tony's interest in them faded when they mentioned their son was a lawyer in Leeds, and their daughter lived a couple of miles away, and she popped in every other day. Far too dangerous. Two more customers with distant relatives presented themselves, and Tony followed the previous path in setting up the wills with Matthew who again failed to notice the now repeated beneficiary, Patrick Baxter. What Tony realised was that he could not continue with this particular route, as sooner or later somebody in the lawyer's office may spot it, and even the hopelessly careless Matthew may stumble across it. He had a new idea which would elevate him faster and produce returns sooner.

Chapter 5

The new idea was almost shelved indefinitely when one Friday morning his calm and controlled exterior was thrown into a major challenge. As he looked across to the entrance door, he saw a more flustered than usual Fiona Cummings marching towards the counter accompanied by an irate looking man. Theresa dealt with her for a few minutes and then left her seat to walk towards Tony's open door where he had been standing, pretending to read a report. Theresa explained that Fiona was in a bit of a flap and, although she didn't have an appointment, would like to see Tony about her accounts, as she was worried about her money.

'Okay, Theresa, give me a few minutes and I will see her. Who is that with her?'

'Oh, that's her son Frank, bit of a thug I think, but he works in the shop. I don't like the look of him.'

Tony closed the door and sat down trying to think what the query might be. He quickly mulled over his transactions with Fiona, and a cold sweat broke out around his neck. He had increased his activity with Fiona in recent months and had been greedy, almost like a child taking more and more sweets until he was sick. His hands became clammy as he calculated that he had increased the stolen funds from around £2,500 to nearly £8,000 in the last few months. It had been too much, and he had taken too great a risk.

He buzzed Theresa on the internal phone and asked her to send them in. Fiona almost stumbled in; her hands fiddled with her vast shopping bag as her sullen looking son walked behind.

'Oh, thank you for seeing me, Tony, I am in so much trouble and don't know what to do.'

'Have a seat, Fiona, and tell me the problem. Is this your son?'

'Yes, this is Frank who helps me on the farm and in the shop. He wants to know more about the business and thinks I'm useless,' she giggled, but Frank remained expressionless and looked at Tony without blinking.

'What appears to be the problem, Fiona?'

'Well the accountant has been, and he says he can't understand the figures. He says that our profits are falling, but our overheads are the same. I just can't understand it because we are as busy as ever, and Frank here has been working overtime,' Fiona explained

'What do you think the problem is?' Tony enquired calmly.

'The accountant says he doesn't like all these accounts, and we should have a business account with the bank to pay everything into.'

'That makes sense, Fiona.'

'Well yes, but we put in one of these computerised tills last month, and the takings don't match the deposits in these books,' Fiona said whilst fishing four dog-eared passbooks out of the overstuffed shopping bag.

'Let me have a look,' Tony said, as the saliva dried in his mouth and his heart rate increased. A computerised till which may show that somewhere between the farm and his desk money had gone missing, and he was a suspect.

'Well, I can see weekly deposits in two of them and less regular deposits in the other two. What does your till tell you?' he enquired.

'Ah, I wish I knew, but the accountant said that the figures don't match.'

Thinking on his feet, and feeling a trickle of sweat wriggling down his back Tony said,

'Do you keep a cash float in the till?'

'Yes.'

'How much is that?'

'Oh, it varies.'

'Do you ever pay for supplies from the till?'

'No.'

'Yes you do, Mam, you always pay for the cakes out of the till,' answered the sullen son now bursting into action.

'Oh yes, we have a local girl who makes the cupcakes, and she likes to be paid cash,' answered Fiona.

'Yeah, and the pork pies from next door,' barked Frank.

'No, that's poor old Ned from the farm next door, and I only pay him cash when he hasn't had a chance to get to the bank. He doesn't like driving so much now since his wife died.'

Tony could feel his heart rate slowing as he could see a bullet dodged.

'Well, there you are Fiona. I am no accountant, but if you take money from the till to pay a supplier, then that will not show up as an overhead which will give you a false figure for the cost of running the business. As you are taking money from the till to buy these things it will show a lower profit in the books. That profit will be in stock. I think you need to open a business account and pay all of the takings into it, and remember to pay all suppliers out of that account, not the till. If you want to pay them cash that is fine as long as you get the cash from the account and show it as a separate transaction.'

'There you are, Frank, I knew there was an explanation. Oh, Tony, I don't know what I would do without you. Why don't you and your family come over for a special high tea at the shop as a thank you, it's really good, and the kids would have plenty to do.'

'That would be lovely, Fiona.'

They got up to leave, and Frank turned to Tony,

'That accountant thinks I've been nicking the money, cheeky bastard.'

Fiona frowned. 'He never said that, Frank. He said it looked like somebody had been helping themselves to our cash.'

'Aye, but he was looking at me.'

Tony smiled as they left and then dropped into his leather chair. He had to stop this particular nest egg and rethink. His wills and probate plan was a good one, and his selection of targets was so far pretty sound. It was, however, an investment, as he had to wait until people died. He wanted to have more now as the thirty grand hit had whetted his appetite and emboldened him to be more ambitious. His emotions, as he reflected, had swayed heavily from fear and shame to excitement and an almost electrical charge when a plan came off. His sense of power and control when enacting his plans was intoxicating. He was orchestrating everyone's moves, and only he knew what was happening. He realised that the visit from Fiona should have been that warning he needed to stop, hide his dishonesty, and never repeat those acts. Instead, it spurred him on to his next more elaborate plan, which would involve a lot more in the way of preparation and a lot more deceit but would give a bigger return.

One of his friends, Bernie Foster, was a financial advisor who had told him so many tales of people not knowing what they had or what they had invested in. This was not news to Tony as he saw that for himself every day in the branch. What intrigued Tony was Bernie's examples of investments that perfectly normal people were persuaded to buy. Bernie himself had been doing the job for more than 20 years and would never advise on a risky investment, but his tales were of messes he had been asked to tidy up. One lady had invested £25,000 of her £30,000 life savings on an internet scheme to buy shares in a tin mine in South America on a 'guaranteed return of 45% after three years'. The company guaranteeing the money was domiciled in Bulgaria and had gone bust. Another man had paid £15,000 betting the price of gold against oil and had lost. It was all he had, and he had no background in that type of market.

Tony would not be looking for that type of investor but a higher worth individual who had money to risk. Georgina Pilkington walked into the branch, and she was perfect for him. She was 55 years old, but looked younger, and had been married three times and divorced... three times. Her choice of husband was fairly consistent in that they were older, well off, and vulnerable to her charms. She probably didn't set out to fail in the marriages, but her excessive spending and demands were always likely to push the husband too far. On the day of her appointment, she walked into his office dressed as though she was going on to a nightclub. Her short mousey hair was immaculately cut, and she wore a tight-fitting silk dress that showed her ample breasts and still shapely figure. Her designer coat hid some of the imperfections that were beginning to catch up with her. The reason for the visit was an enquiry about a mortgage for her daughter who was getting married and wanted to buy a house. Georgina was apparently not too impressed with her son-in-law to be and wanted the house in her daughter's name only. She would pay the deposit if they agreed to that.

Tony went through the mortgage rates but quickly moved on to her status.

'So, Georgina, is it alright if I call you Georgina?'

'Oh please do, Tony,' she said flirtatiously, looking at his nameplate.

'I see you don't have any investments with us, how are your investments doing?' he enquired.

'Absolute shit, Tony, pardon my French, almost nothing these days. I really don't know what to do.'

'Maybe I can help; do you mind telling me what you have?'

'No, not at all. I have a bond with RBS which matures in two months' time, but it was connected to the stock market or something, and it isn't going to pay anything. I will just be glad to get my money back.'

'How much is that?' he asked with pen poised.

'One hundred and fifty grand.'

'Anything else?' he asked writing down the first figure.

'Yes, I have a cash ISA with sixty grand, an offshore bond with two hundred and fifty grand, and my second husband's shares with the company he used to work for. They say they are worth half a million, but I only get a few grand a year dividend. Oh, and I've got a couple of cottages that pay rent.'

'Wow, that's pretty impressive, Georgina. Do you have something in mind by way of investment?' Tony gently mused.

'Not really, but I am fed up with the peanuts I get now. One of my friends says she gets more income with much less money invested.'

Tony felt the vibration of the spider sensing a fly stepping on to its web.

'Well, I am afraid I can only offer you a little better return here at the society, but I can introduce you to an independent colleague who may be able to do more with some of your money. However, you would have to be prepared to take a risk. He doesn't work for the society.'

'Take a risk? I have been married three times; I am used to taking a risk,' she replied laughing.

'Well look, when your bond matures why don't we put £100,000 in our top earning account, which will give you a little more interest than anyone else at the moment and see if my associate can do something much better with the other £50k?'

'Sounds good, Tony, what is his name?'

'Patrick Baxter,' he replied, without breaking stride in his thought process and without a plan. He just knew he would think of one.

Chapter 6

After Georgina had gone his mind found a new gear. This was a chance to move into a different league and produce instant cash without waiting for people to die. What he had to do was develop this new identity to deal with people from a safe distance and persuade them to invest with him for a large return, but to expect to lose at some point. Nothing should be traceable to him, other than a recommendation. He could not use this as widely as he could with those conveniently dying as those likely to live may bump into each other and put two and two together.

The following few days completed his plan for Georgina. He would set up a business by buying a limited company off the shelf and renaming it One Life Investments Limited. He would issue shares in the name of Patrick Baxter and three fictitious European names to make it sound like an international company by background. Patrick Baxter would ring Georgina and say he was rarely in the UK as most of his work was abroad, and therefore could not meet her. He would set up a website, which he was capable of doing thanks to a local course at the college in Harrogate five years ago. He would do everything online with no access addresses and only his mobile phone or an email address for contact, both registered to Patrick Baxter. Method established, he now had to decide the detail. Georgina would give him £50,000 in exchange for a fake certificate that he would knock up on his MacBook Pro, and he would pay her for a couple of years and then tell her it was failing, that he was fighting to recover the investment, and then break the news it was lost. This was riskier but more reward often is. It also meant that the money would be his to play with from the start of the arrangement.

One night when everyone had left the branch, he picked up the mobile rented in his false name and rang Georgina. When she answered, he spoke with a much-practised private school accent.

'Oh hello, could I speak to Georgina Pilkington please?'

'Speaking.'

'Ah, nice to talk to you; my name is Patrick Baxter. I gather you may have been expecting my call?'

'Are you the friend of Tony from the building society?' she enquired.

'More colleagues than friends I would say, but yes he gave me your number.'

What followed was fifteen minutes of conversation where Tony amazed himself at not only keeping up the accent but also his control of the conversation. They talked about backgrounds and experiences, with Tony inventing a fraught and frantic lifestyle with a growing number of people demanding his time. When he felt it was appropriate, he said,

'I get the picture, Georgina, but I would not advise you to invest in anything with me that you cannot afford to lose, so keep the bulk of your investments in safer waters. You will get 1 or 2% on a deposit account and bonds and maybe 4 or 5% with some stock market-based products. The last private bond I did returned 10%'.

'Sounds great, Patrick, I will have some of that.'

'That one is closed, but we have another coming up in the next few weeks if you are interested. However, please remember there are greater risks attached to these products, and they are not guaranteed by the UK authorities like your other investments.'

'That doesn't worry me, Patrick, there is no fun without risk is there?' she said with a giggle.

'Well, if you are sure,' he responded with a teasing tone.

'My money comes in at the end of next month, so if it is available then I would want to do it.'

'Why don't I give you a call in the middle of next month and let us see what we can do.'

'Lovely, look forward to hearing from you, Patrick.'

When he put the phone down, Tony felt that surge of adrenalin pulse through his veins as he had entered this new league of deception. This was undoubted fraud where he could not pretend he was doing something that he was entitled to do or something a little shade of grey. This was a dark shade of black with dire consequences if he was discovered, but he felt no remorse at that point or desire for safety. He was developing a Jekyll and Hyde twin personality. During his normal day job and his dealings with his family and friends he was the very amiable Dr Jekyll but now, always in the background lurked the darker Mr Hyde, watching and waiting for prey to wander in front of him where he would emerge and pounce.

The night of the phone call he arrived home and was met with his wife Jemma, who kissed him when he walked in, took his briefcase from his hand, and said,

'You had better pop straight up and see Anna; she has been waiting for you all night and is upset.'

'What's the problem?' he enquired with a worried look.

'Oh, she has been bullied at school, and one of the teachers said something to her about her hair being too long. She doesn't want me to speak to the teacher or the kids, but she said Daddy would know what to do,' Jemma said, looking up to the sky in mock irritation.

Tony opened Anna's bedroom door, and as he did so, she jumped off her bed and ran into his arms crying.

'Oh, Daddy, I am so unhappy,' she blurted out amongst the tears.

'Now then, what's all this about, Peanut? Let's sit on the bed and sort it out.'

Anna proceeded to tell him the sorry tale of two girls in her class who said that her long black hair made her look like a witch from Harry Potter and that she should buy a broomstick. Then when she confided in her teacher, she said that her hair was very long and that maybe she could have it trimmed as it must be a big job to wash it and keep it clean. Tony thought for a while, stroked his daughter's long hair, and said,

'Well now. So you look like a witch because of your hair, is that right?'

'That's what they said Daddy, and the teacher wants me to cut it so I must look like one,' Anna said as the sobs increased.

Tony smiled at his daughter, then picked up his iPad and using Google he pulled up pictures of Julia Roberts,

Angelina Jolie, Emily Blunt, and Keira Knightly, and several more with long black hair.

'Wow, look at these witches, Anna. They seem to be happy, don't they? Now if I was a girl and I had to sit with a beautiful girl in class who had long black hair that made her look even more beautiful I don't think I would like it. So maybe I would try and make her feel bad and maybe even persuade her to cut her hair, so she looked slightly less beautiful,' he said calmly whilst looking into her deep brown wide-open eyes.

'Do you think that is why they said it, Daddy?'

'I bet it is,' he said, continuing to stroke the flowing locks.

'Yes, but why did the teacher tell me to cut my hair, Daddy?'

'I'm not sure she did, did she? Sometimes grown-ups try to please everybody and end up pleasing nobody. She was probably trying to say something that would keep the peace. The only girl in your class I am bothered about is you, Peanut. You should keep your long hair, and if people don't like it, I think it is just that they are jealous of you. You have lots of friends and family who love your hair and you.'

Anna moved closer, put both arms around him and said through fresh tears,

'Oh Daddy, I knew you would know what to do, and you would fix it for me. You always do. I love you so much, Daddy.'

'I love you too, Peanut,' was his reply as he squeezed her gently.

Yes, he remembered that moment very well as the

warmth and love that he felt for his daughter brought that familiar deep satisfaction that he often felt when with his family. What he remembered most of that moment was not the feeling of Anna burying her head into his chest, but his own tears squeezing from his eyes like unwelcome guests at a party. The confused emotions that surfaced for the first time as his Dr Jekyll wanted to be on his own and maybe realised that Mr Hyde was taking over. He never wanted his precious family to meet or even know of the other personality.

In the days and weeks that followed he moved on from his dilemma and when the cheque for £50,000 arrived from Georgina, he paid it into his newly opened One Life Ltd bank account. He diarised a date three months from then when he would pay Georgina her first return on the investment as part of the longer game. As he floated through these memories at his desk, he recognised Georgina as a point of no return; a step too far if he was ever to find his way back to his comfortable, normal life and the warmth and security of his family. Having taken that step, he was caught in the grip of greed and the exercise of power over those he encountered as well as the excitement of the world of deceit. That world had great danger, but gave him a feeling of strength along with the control and a glimpse of a life he would never be able to afford on his salary. Why should the intellectually inferior upper middle classes that he met have all of the trappings of success that would be denied to him? He was creating a separate world where he could enjoy them and maybe one day he would tell

Jemma, and she would accept the position and join him in the enjoyment of the proceeds of his actions. Even as he remembered that thought at his desk, he realised it was naive and deluded, and that Jemma and her family would never accept what he had been doing.

Maybe it was that delusion that had allowed him to crank up the thefts and to develop an almost unquenchable thirst for it. In any event, the next big one appeared within weeks as he was introduced to Miss Helen Marchant, a wealthy spinster who lived in an affluent area of York. Matthew Barker rang one afternoon with his usual chirpy tone.

'Hello, Tony, old man, how are tricks?'

'Oh, fair to middling.'

'Well, I am very conscious of all the work you send me, so I have a bit of reciprocation for you in the shape of one Helen Marchant, a client of the firm. Frightful woman really, but obscenely wealthy. Her father was a stockbroker who made squillions back in the day and left her his fortune when he croaked years ago. She has never married and spends her time falling out with people,' he explained.

'Sounds dreadful, where do we come in?' he enquired.

'Well, I know you can't be an executor in wills for the society members, but she isn't, and I thought you could be an executor with me and help me on the estate when she goes to meet her maker, which might be quite soon I gather as she has a heart that is hanging on by a thread. You will get paid for your work and to be honest I don't want one of my partners involved. I don't really get on with any of them, and one or two think I am a bit of a prat,' he ended with a nervous laugh.

'Okay, Matthew, when shall we see her?'

'Tomorrow at 2 pm if that's alright with you? Not sure how much time we have, what with her health and everything.'

The spider's tingle was felt again.

Chapter 7

Matthew picked up Tony at 12.30 pm, and they stopped for a quick lunch before driving to the imposing property of Helen Marchant, a large Victorian house standing in its own grounds, guarded by a two metre wall and electronic gates that opened to give access to the gravelled drive, and an impressive set of double front doors facing them as they parked. Matthew pulled a large metal handle on the side of the door and heard a dull bell sound. After a minute or so the housekeeper, Mrs Gamble, opened the left-hand door and bid them a good afternoon.

'We are here to see Miss Marchant for a 2 o'clock appointment,' explained Matthew.

'Yes, please come in and take a seat in the drawing room,' answered the rather chunky middle-aged woman.

The drawing room was large, with period furniture and a huge bay window overlooking part of the garden. In the garden, a man was working. He looked to be about the same age as the housekeeper and quite possibly her husband. Tony noticed that there were no photographs of family or indeed the owner. There were a few paintings on the walls of country scenes, fox hunting, and one of an old serious looking toff that he imagined was the wealthy father. They were in the room for a full ten minutes before the housekeeper returned, asked them if they would like a cup of tea, and said that Miss Marchant would be with them soon but whispered that she was not having a good day and they should be careful.

Finally, the door opened again and in walked the lady of the house who was tall, thin, and frail. She wore expensive clothes that were obviously old; her long grey hair was neatly tied into a bun, and she walked with heavy reliance upon a stick in her right hand. That hand was bone-like, thin with dark blue prominent veins standing proud of the almost translucent flesh.

'Good afternoon, gentlemen, you will have to forgive my lateness. I am not very strong, I am afraid. I am also not very patient, so I would be obliged if we can deal with matters quickly as I tire easily.'

Matthew stumbled around, not sure whether to assist the old lady or stand aside to avoid being whacked with the stick. Tony took the lead,

'Hello, Miss Marchant, I am Tony Needham, and this is Matthew Barker. We gather you want to change your will, and we are here to take your instructions to do so. We are aware of your health issues and will do whatever you wish us to do. If you do feel tired, we can stop and come back another time entirely to suit you.'

She looked at them both quizzically before responding,

'Yes, well I am not dead yet, and I will tell you if I need any mollycoddling thank you. Have you got my current will?'

Matthew fumbled about in his briefcase and produced her 20-year-old will in his slightly shaking right hand saying,

'Yes, it is here, your… err Miss Marchant,' as he almost called her 'Your Ladyship'. Tony suppressed a smile at his friend's performance and saw how intimidated he was in the company of an aggressive wealthy woman.

'Tell me where everything is going under that will,' Miss Marchant barked.

Matthew opened the document, waffled through some of the terms, and under the duress of much tutting and head shaking from his client, finally gave the information he had been asked to provide.

'So, my sister was to get half of everything. The Methodist Church was to get most of the rest, and there were gifts to my nephew and two nieces. Is that correct?'

'Yes, that is about the size of it,' answered Matthew

'Well, my sister is dead, and I haven't heard from her children in ten years, so I don't want them getting a penny. I want the house to go to the National Trust, but on the condition they leave it as it is and maintain it in the family name for posterity. I want my housekeeper, Mrs Gamble, to receive £100,000 and her husband, the gardener, to receive £50,000. The rest can go to charities, and I am open to suggestions on that. Is that clear?'

'Yes, I think so,' answered Matthew.

'So, what do you need to know?' Miss Marchant asked in a semi-hostile tone.

'We need to have your choice of executors…. that is the people who will deal with your estate and…'

'I know what executors are, young man,' she spat out at Matthew.

'Yes, yes of course, but you need to choose at least two and the powers you will give them. It would be useful for us to have an inventory of an estate the size of this so that we can deal with it efficiently when you… err when the… I mean…,' Matthew spluttered…

'When I am dead,' she completed the sentence

'Well yes, I suppose that is the top and bottom of it,' Matthew added with a small bead of sweat rolling gently down his right temple.

'Very well, when can you start? My death is not imminent, although I have been warned it could happen soon and I want everything tied up, so I do not need to think about the details.'
Tony sensed he had more of a chance of a connection than the hapless Matthew and seized the moment.

'Matthew and I could be your professional executors, or you could choose your housekeeper or someone else. The point of professional executors is that you know they are trained for the job, and although not related to you they are not beneficiaries either and are less likely to do anything other than your wishes. It would give wide powers so that we or whoever you choose can delay sales of assets if it is the best thing to do and to make sure there is no selling of your family belongings cheaply.'

'I certainly would not want Mr or Mrs Gamble trying to deal with the estate as they sometimes have difficulty dealing with the shopping. I have no relatives that I wish to have involved and no close friends to speak of. You two will have to do,' she said tartly.

'Very well, Miss Marchant, my colleague Matthew will draw up the first draft, and if Saturday is convenient, I will call and make a start on the inventory. Either you or Mrs Gamble can show me around,' Tony offered.

'Yes, that is fine, and if you will excuse me, I am a little tired, and when you have finished your tea Mrs Gamble will show you out,' she said, getting up a little unsteadily and walking slowly to the door. When they got back into the car, Matthew said,

'What a frightful cow. Glad you were there Tony as she frightened the pants off me. Reminded me of my prep school headmistress who was trained by the Gestapo. Fancy a drink?'

They stopped off at a nearby pub, and Matthew explained that he would like Tony to do all of the legwork and be paid an hourly rate that the firm would charge out. Matthew would charge £250 per hour and charge Tony out at £150 per hour as an outside consultant. When it came to the probate after the client's death, they would come to a similar arrangement. Tony would work at weekends or evenings so as to not interfere with his job or alert his employers that he had this second income. In the pub, Tony also disclosed his latest plan.

'So, Matthew, there are dozens of care homes in the Harrogate area, and I thought we could offer a surgery appointment system where we go in and give residents advice on making or revising wills, investments, and setting up trusts. We could say the initial advice is free, but if they wanted to use the service there would be a discount or something like that... what do you think?'

'Sounds very interesting. I am always under pressure to hit my costs targets, so anything that helps me there takes some of that pressure off,' Matthew replied, wide-eyed.

'Well, I contacted a dozen or so, and four have said they were interested as long as there was no hard sell. I spoke to my regional manager, and he liked the idea to raise further investment into the society.'

This was a plan in Tony's head that was evolving. They would go to the care homes of the well-heeled and keep his employers happy by introducing some business for them. Matthew's firm would like the additional business and all of the time he would be able to spot the unsupported target and move in. He would be hiding in plain sight. Matthew now relied upon him so much that he would sign anything Tony put in front of him so that the possibilities were endless. What he liked was that this was another crop being planted as he prepared to harvest the Marchant crop which was ripening in front of his very eyes.

The following day he told Jemma that he was going to be working some weekends and evenings but she was to keep this to herself, as technically, he should not work for anyone without his employer's permission. Jemma looked startled and asked why he would take any risk at all and that they had a good life without any extra money. He told her that good was not enough, that he wanted to book special holidays for her and the kids, and he wanted his children to have everything that he was not able to have and as much as anybody else's children get. He was irritated with Jemma because she did not seem to feel the same way, and at one point he raised his voice to make the point, which caused her to step back and ask if he was alright. When he reflected about it now, he realised that his irritation with his wife was that she was inadvertently removing one of his excuses for being drawn to these dark deeds by making it clear that he did not need to do it for the children. Subconsciously he knew that his wife was right and that he was drawn by the deed itself. This was why he could hardly sleep on the nights leading up to his next visit to Miss Marchant; he was too excited. What he didn't realise was that a totally unexpected and unpredictable opportunity was going to present itself that did not require the death of Helen Marchant or the delay of probate.

Chapter 8

At 9.00 am on that Saturday he drove up to the Marchant property, and although he did not know what he was looking for, he was sure he would recognise it when he saw it. He was anyway earning some legitimate extra money and would be able to splash some cash on his family.

Mrs Gamble answered the door and explained that her employer was still in bed but had asked her to show him around, apart from the master suite upstairs where Miss Marchant would be getting ready at some point. The tour was indeed interesting as a lesson in how the other half lived. Starting with downstairs, he was shown the living room, the dining hall, the library, the familiar drawing room, and then the huge kitchen with several rooms off for storage of food and kitchen equipment. There was then a sunroom with a conservatory attached and doors out into the well-manicured gardens which ran to several acres. Upstairs there were five additional bedrooms to the master suite and a loft the size of the footprint of the house where years of family items were stored. In the grounds, there were two additional buildings which stored all the garden vehicles and equipment and could easily be turned into family homes themselves.

The house had been in the family for many years and would be worth millions, given its location. The room that interested him most, as it turned out, was the vault that was positioned behind the Library wall. Mrs Gamble pressed a concealed black button and the wall holding one of the mahogany bookshelves slid to the right under the strength of a noisy ancient electric motor. Once fully open, a six-foot-high metal door with a brass wheel in the middle faced Tony.

'Bit like something out of James Bond, isn't it Mr Needham,' giggled Mrs Gamble. 'There's no money in there, just loads of old papers,' she added.

'How do we get in, Miss Moneypenny?' Tony flirted to Mrs Gamble's amusement.

'Here is the key,' she said, handing over an eight-inch iron key for the lock below the wheel. Once engaged, a loud click meant the wheel could be turned releasing the six brass bolts holding the door closed and entry into a room of several shelves illuminated by one hanging light bulb.

'There you go, help yourself, and I will bring you some tea. She says all of the deeds to all of the properties are in here, and share certificates and such. She keeps the bank stuff in her desk in her dressing room upstairs, and she says she will talk to you about that... rather you than me,' she added laughing as she walked towards the door.

The vault smelt stuffy and a little damp. Shelves on the left-hand side had cardboard boxes with brass corners that may not have been touched in years. A gritty dust had settled on them, and the spiders of many generations had left their decayed webs all around them. When he pulled some of them from the top shelf, a cloud of dust and debris fell like a slow-moving fog onto his jacket before settling on his shoes. The first box was entitled Share documentation

for International Chemicals Limited. Inside the box were
several share certificates and some correspondence dating
back to 1957. The most recent letter was April 1974 and
related to the last acquisition, the purchase of 200 ordinary
shares by Bostock, Ronson, and Carpenter, Stock Brokers.
The next four boxes contained a mixture of certificates,
letters, notes from Bernard Marchant, and some leaflets
relating to the various companies. It was clear that Bernard
Marchant was the father of Miss Marchant and clearly was
a dealer in many financial matters as well as being very
wealthy. Tony would have to log all of these items and
then research their value. The right-hand side shelves had
black tin boxes of various sizes, but no outside labels. There
were six boxes that varied from 18 inches by 10 inches to
the larger size of a few inches bigger. Three of them had
keys still in the locks, and when Tony opened them, he
found personal letters from Bernard Marchant to a number
of people as well as their replies. One was from Coutts
Bank dated the 15th of March, 1964, which read,

Dear Mr Marchant,
Re: The Haven, Nile Street, Penzance Cornwall
*I write to confirm your instructions to issue a banker's draft in
the sum of £22,500 in the name of your solicitors, Baylish and
Cooper, in respect of the purchase of this property which I understand
will be completed later in the month. Your deposit account has been
debited with this sum, and the draft can be collected from the branch
at any time to suit your convenience.*
Yours faithfully,
Derek Bruce, Manager

The figure of £22,500 was clearly a great deal then and a sign of the kind of money available to this family. Did they still own the property? On the bottom shelf lay the largest black box, which was three feet long and two feet high, giving the appearance of a treasure chest. It was locked and again covered in long-standing dust. Standing at the back of the vault were five oil paintings leaning against each other. Tony flicked through them and saw two Victorian portraits of grim-looking men in winged collars, two landscapes and a very dusty scene of sheep and cows. He took out his mobile phone and photographed each one separately and took close-ups of the signatures. He also photographed the various boxes and then took out his large notebook from his briefcase to start the arduous task of listing all that was available to him. Mrs Gamble returned with the tea and biscuits and said,

'Miss Marchant is up and about and will join you shortly,' winking as she left.

Half an hour later, in walked the owner looking a little better than at their last meeting, but still relying heavily on the stick for balance.

'Good Morning, Mr Needhurst, I hope you have found what you need?'

'It's Needham, Miss Marchant. Tony Needham.'

'As you wish,' she replied indifferently.

'There are some boxes here without keys,' he commented, whilst getting to his feet from the chair he had placed in the vault.

'Yes, my Grandmother's jewellery is in one of them,

and the big one has the deeds to the family properties,' she replied.

'I wonder if I could open them to make a list, with you here of course.'

'I don't let anyone have access to those boxes, Mr .... sorry what did you say your name was?'

'Needham, but you can call me Tony if it is easier.'

'No, thank you, Mr Needham will do nicely although I shall need to write it down, I think,' she said haughtily

'So, does anyone but you have access to the boxes?' he enquired.

'Certainly not,' was the sharp response.

'Unfortunately, I cannot catalogue everything unless I can see it and the difficulty is that if I don't do it, there will be no record of your possessions at the time of your death which would leave the estate open to dishonesty, unless your insurers or bank have a list,' he confidently pronounced.

'I have never trusted banks and nor did my father. I trust insurers even less,' she barked.

'Well, it is entirely up to you, and I can come back another time if that is better for you.'

'Oh God no, I want this done as soon as possible. I shall fetch the keys as nobody knows where they are either,' she said, as she turned and stomped as fast as her failing limbs would take her. Whilst she was gone Tony assimilated the information at his disposal and wrote the following in his notebook:

1. There were no separate lists of assets held outside of the house by banks, insurers or anyone else.

2. Nobody, other than Miss Marchant, had access to the

locked boxes and presumably no knowledge of their contents.

3. The family wealth appeared to have been accumulated by the deceased father with perhaps little of his acumen being passed on to his daughter.

4. Subject to what was in the boxes and through his research there was no countercheck as to assets and unlikely to be anyone other than Miss Marchant who had information. Was her knowledge of the assets extensive?

The familiar rush coursing through his veins with that flush of excitement was becoming a narcotic to him. The treasure was here; he just had to find it and then discover a way of spiriting some of it away. He continued to list the items he had access to when Miss Marchant returned and handed him a set of rusted keys attached to a wooden peg.

'Here you are, please be as quick as you can,' she instructed.

Tony tried the smaller boxes first and finally married up the correct keys and locks. The first was indeed a box of jewellery which comprised diamond, emerald, and sapphire rings, as well as necklaces, bracelets, and pendants. He was not an expert and assumed he was looking at the real thing rather than fake stones.

'What I propose is that I set the items out on the floor and photograph them all together, so you have a record of what is in this box and then take individual shots of each piece so that you know what is here,' he explained.

'Very well,' she agreed impatiently.

Tony deliberately took his time to show both his attention

to detail and also to tire his watcher. He was thinking whilst he was working, but he was pretty sure he would not be stealing any jewellery. He knew little about it, would have to sell it, and then risk a trace back to him. It was also an obvious choice for a thief, and if he could show scrupulously honest behaviour here it would assist in the trust he may need later. If there ever was an investigation on other matters the total honesty in relation to very easy theft jewellery would make him a less likely suspect.

'I can email these photos to you, Miss Marchant; do you have an email address?'

'Do I what?' she replied with an expression that looked as though she had been asked if she had a criminal record.

'An email address, the internet, electronic communication?' he pretended to fumble.

'I have no interest in that modern, lazy way of communication. If people want to communicate with me they can come and see me or write a letter,' she stated with conviction.

Better and better Tony thought to himself. This self-imposed righteous isolation was an aide to whatever plan he would develop. After another half an hour, Miss Marchant's exasperation had reached its zenith, and she looked at Tony and said,

'Right, you have photographed the jewellery so if you lock that up and give me the key you can look at the rest on your own as the other boxes only hold papers and deeds. Quickly now, I need to go and rest,' she ordered.

Tony did as she asked, replaced the jewellery, locked the box, and watched his prey walk unsteadily out of the room.

The other boxes were his, and his pulse raced again. He had a strong feeling that something in those boxes would offer itself to him; he just had to find it.

Chapter 9

The clock seemed to be ticking louder on his wall in his office as he broke off from his backward journey to see that the time was 7.48 am. Only 7.48 am. Why was time going so slowly, when his mind was racing so quickly through weeks, months, years… time that was racing and events happening so quickly? There was still over an hour to opening time, and it seemed more than enough time to reflect on all of these events.

It was easy to go back to that day in the vault because the emotions were so fresh that he could almost smell the stale air in the small enclosure of the giant safe, the leather of the furniture in the library, and even the waxed paper of some of the older deeds. The lock to the deeds box was stiff, and at first, he thought it was the wrong key, but then he realised it had not been opened for years, maybe many years. In one of the smaller boxes, he had come across the death certificate of Bernard Marchant, which told him he had died of coronary heart disease on the 24th of July, 1977, at the age of 76. He imagined that his daughter may be around the same age now and that her genes had the same weakness. He also wondered if the deed box had been opened since that time as he forced the key until the resistance of rust and inactivity gave way and the box was open.

It was full and surprisingly free of dust due to the skill of the workman who had made it and the seal it provided. There were several bundles of deeds all wrapped in pink tape. He pulled them all out and counted fifteen piles of documents, some larger than others. They all represented properties and told, in some cases, the ancient history of ownership. The house he was sitting in had the largest collection of documents, which dated back to the eighteenth century, and the older ones were handwritten on giant single waxed paper with a hand-drawn plan showing the land and buildings. At the bottom was a vivid red seal used to complete the deal. The earliest document was for the land only as part of a much bigger piece of land and had been bought for 40 guineas. The house itself was built sometime between 1860 and 1872, which was the first time it was mentioned as a house. Bernard Marchant had bought the property in 1954 for £19,800 a very small proportion of its worth today.

Tony recorded every property and the purchase dates in his note pad but was drawn to the small bundle that told the history of The Haven in Penzance, Cornwall. He already knew the purchase price and the date of purchase from the letter from Coutts, but here was its history. He was lost in detail and unaware of the passage of time until Mrs Gamble interrupted him to ask if he would like some lunch as it was now past 3 o'clock.

'3… 3? Oh My God, I am supposed to be picking my son up, and I'm already late.' He quickly bundled everything up into their boxes, locked them, and ran to his car. 'Tell Miss Marchant I have the keys and guarantee their safety, but I must dash. I will return them tonight if she wishes or keep them until my next visit. I will ring you tonight, Mrs Gamble.' He quickly tapped the house telephone number into his contacts on his phone and then ran to his car with Mrs Gamble looking on.

His heart was pounding as he raced to the school where the children's party was taking place, having agreed with Jemma in the morning that he would collect his son at 2, and here he was still driving at 3.20. He tried Jemma's number, but she didn't pick up, and he almost crashed into a stationary vehicle at the traffic lights as he looked down to find the school number. There was no answer from that number either, and fear and dread began to wash over him. What might have happened, where might Toby be? Might he have gone out with the other children and not said anything when the other parents left? He was five years old and could have been picked up by anyone.

As he pulled into the school car park, there was no sign of anyone. He jumped out of the car and ran, panic-stricken, into the empty classrooms shouting out his son's name. The anxiety was turning to panic as the fear of Jemma's disappointment was replaced with unimaginable images of his beloved son being abducted. It is amazing how the mind can conjure up horrific detailed pictures in just a few seconds. The horror of blind searching in the street, police visits, sleepless nights of terror, all flooded into his head.

'Mr Needham, is that you?' called one of the teachers as Tony turned quickly.

'Toby is in the Head Teacher's study,' said the voice calmly.

'Oh my God, thank you and sorry. Where is the office?'

A slightly censorious finger pointed towards the door a few yards away, and Tony briskly walked towards it, knocked and entered.

'Ah, Mr Needham, we imagined you were detained and couldn't raise you on your home number. We don't seem to have your mobile number, I am afraid,' said the surprisingly understanding Bruce Whelan, a man he had spoken to only briefly before.

'I cannot tell you how sorry I am, my watch stopped whilst I was working, and I completely lost track of time,' he said pulling his cuff over the merrily ticking watch.

'Oh, don't worry about it, happens all the time and we have contingency plans in place. I might even forget to tell Mrs Needham for a tenner,' he chuckled.

Toby was fine, but a little disappointed he hadn't been allowed to go home with one of the other kids. Tony's blood pressure was returning to normal and his position of a few minutes ago, when he would have gladly gone to prison for knowledge of his son's safety, was being replaced with concern that he might have upset his plans for Miss Marchant by leaving so hurriedly and still having her keys.

'Don't tell your Mum I was late, Toby.'

'Okay, Daddy.'

As they arrived home, Toby ran from the car to the front door where his mother was waiting.

'Mummy, Mummy, Daddy was late collecting me, and I had to wait with the teacher. Daddy has to pay him ten pounds or something.'

Tony smiled at Jemma, who was scowling back, but his thoughts were now elsewhere.

Chapter 10

Very surprisingly, Miss Marchant was not concerned at the speed of his departure or his retention of the keys. Mrs Gamble said she thought her employer felt it helped her not having to be disturbed next time he came. That next time was the following Saturday, by which time he had done land registry searches on all the properties listed in his note pad. Of the 15 properties, two had been sold some years ago, and one had been placed in trust for a charity that seemed to support the Conservative Party. Ten properties were registered in the name of Bernard Marchant and one in the name of Elizabeth Edmondson, who lived in Chester at the property address. The one property that had not been registered was The Haven. Tony had researched on the internet, and that area had not been subject to compulsory registration at the time of purchase in 1964. He had read that although an Act of Parliament in 1925 had made a common policy of centrally registering titles of property on sales and purchases, this was brought in over a long period of years, and some rural areas were very slow in participating. It appeared that this area of Cornwall was one of them. It meant there was no central system for checking on this property and, more importantly, on who owned it. That proof was the bundle of documents that he had seen, and crucially very few others knew about. It was the only proof.

He had to find out if Miss Marchant knew about it and if there was a stream of information back to her. If the property were let to a tenant, then presumably she would be getting rent. She might also be paying for services through her account, and her ownership of the property would be traceable through that, making his embryonic plan very dangerous. Having settled into the library again, he heard Mrs Gamble open the door and the clanking of her tray carrying the tea and biscuits.

'There you are, Mr Needham, that will keep you going for a while,' she said with her familiar cheery style.

'Thank you, Mrs G; is there any chance I can see Miss Marchant today?' he said, turning in his chair and smiling.

'Oh Lady Penelope is having her bath at the moment, but I will ask,' she laughed the end of the sentence, and Tony realised she must be very comfortable with him to liken her employer to the puppet out of Thunderbirds. He also wondered how she could tolerate working for such an unpleasant woman, but perhaps she was short on choice. Tony worked for the next hour or so going through documentation and in particular looking for any trust documents. The rich were prone to creating trusts to preserve their assets from death taxes, and he needed to know if there was more than the one trust that he had discovered so far. Perhaps the properties were all held in this way. He could not find anything that suggested the existence of a further property trust and was scratching his forehead when Mrs Gamble came in and said,

'Miss Marchant will see you in the Drawing Room in ten minutes.'

'Oh, that's great, Mrs G, you are a diamond – lovely tea, by the way.' Tony rehearsed his approach as he counted the minutes. When he was satisfied he had all eventualities covered, he walked across the hallway and knocked on the Drawing Room door. After a louder, second knock, he heard the frail but assertive voice of his host asking him to come in. He sat in a dark red leather chair facing Miss Marchant who was positioned near the large marble fireplace, sitting on a delicate nineteenth-century sofa.

'Thank you for seeing me, Miss Marchant, and again apologies for my sudden departure last week. I was late collecting my young son.'

She waved away the apology wordlessly and showed no interest in his mini-crisis or child. Tony opened up his now detailed notes and putting them quickly in order said,

'I have completed a search of your late father's deed box and come up with a list of fourteen sets of deeds, of which twelve seem to be current properties held in the estate. Does that seem about right to you?' he enquired, with heart racing.

'I really don't know, Mr, err, and err.'

'Needham.'

'Yes, quite so, Mr Needham. It sounds about right. My father did buy and sell a lot of property in a time when it was not so fashionable to do so.'

'Your father appears to have placed one property, 27 Hill Towers in Maidstone, Kent, in trust; however I have not been able to find a trust document.'

'Yes, I know about that one. My father was conned by Lord Garfield to invest in the Tory Party in exchange for an Honours list reward. He decided to put one of his properties in trust to give an income to the Party, but nothing came of it. He did not receive his reward and tried to get out of the trust, but the lawyers said he couldn't. All the rents go to the beneficiary, as far as I know.'

'There is another property in the name of Elizabeth Edmondson; the deeds are here but not the Land Registry certificate which is the true deed of ownership.'

'That property need not concern you and does not form part of the Estate,' she answered tartly.

'Do you know about income from the other properties?' he enquired gently.

'Well, I get rents or interest or something, and that is controlled by the accountant who sends me a sum of money every month. They pay it into my bank account.'

'Do you have anything from them to explain how the sum is calculated?' he said hopefully.

'Yes, they send me a statement every year and complete my tax returns, as well as charging me a fortune. It is a Mr Roberts from Gillow, Makepeace in York who does it. Tedious little man; always wears a brown suit and is always fidgeting.'

'May I see the returns?' Tony asked.

'Why do you need to see my returns?' she said with a slightly raised voice, but Tony was ready for that one.

'I may not need to see them, but then I would be guessing at the assets, and there may be problems in the future on the probate. Nothing better for solicitors than lots of unanswered questions and lots of enquiries to make; however, if you are uncomfortable we can leave it.'

He knew his prey well by now, and she huffily rose from her seat and went to a large oak desk whilst taking a small bunch of old keys from her handbag. She opened the bottom right-hand side drawer and after some fumbling produced a handful of plastic covered documents. When she gave them to Tony he could see the accountant's name on each, and he flicked through them whilst she watched him carefully. They did not identify the properties but did confirm she was receiving rents, dividends and interest on investments as well as a small private pension. In the last completed year, she had received an income of just under £227,000. What he didn't know was if anything came from The Haven.

'Do you have an account into which the various sums are received?' he probed.

'I suppose you want to see that as well.'

'It may help.'

Another trip to the desk and she returned with her bank statements, bound in a Coutts Bank leather file.

'This will take me a while, and I wonder if I can borrow these and work in the library so as not to disturb you?'

'Very well, but don't take too long,' she replied, whilst dismissing him with a hand gesture.

Tony felt as though he had triumphed in having this key to the income streams and the answer to the Cornish property. Was there some clue in the documents he now had? As he opened the door, he almost knocked Mrs Gamble over as she had obviously been listening at the door. She quickly composed herself and walked back to the library with him. Once inside, she closed the door and said,

'You asked her about Lizzie Edmondson, didn't you?'

'Elizabeth Edmondson, yes I did.'

'You better not do that again. Lizzie Edmondson was her father's mistress, and she can't bear to hear her name mentioned. She blames Lizzie for her mother's death. Some say she died from a broken heart. She was a lovely lady. Anyway, the Old Man bought her the house years ago and used to visit her regularly there. She's dead now, of course. Don't know who lives there now.'

'Do you know if any of the properties would be in trusts?' he asked, now seeing another line of enquiry.

'No, Mr Marchant liked to keep his money around him. He put that one you mentioned in one of those trusts, but he liked to keep everything close to his chest. We don't think he declared everything to the taxman. She might have a mouthful of plums, but she isn't whiter than white either. They say that they kept lots of stuff off the probate so that the tax bill was reduced. I don't know really... hey, I shouldn't be saying any of this to you. Don't you say you heard it from me,' she said, colouring a little and raising her hand to her mouth.

'Muriel - it is Muriel, isn't it? I hope you don't mind me calling you by your first name. I promise you that anything you say to me will remain between us. You are the only bright light for me when I come here, and the last thing I would do is upset you.'

'Oh, thanks very much, Mr Needham.'

'Tony, please.'

'Oh thanks very much, Tony,' she said with a giggle.

So there it was. The father was a tax dodger with a mistress. The daughter did not trust anyone to have access to her information or records, except her accountant whom she does not like and with whom she is unlikely to have a strong relationship. The key then is what do the accountants know, and does Miss Marchant know anything about The Haven or remember it. The answer came about 45 minutes later, after a search of the bank accounts and a more thorough reading of the accountant's documents. There was no breakdown of the monthly payment into the Marchant account other than simple statements of sums that were described as rents, other sums described as interest, and then deductions for work done. The outgoings showed insurance payments and some council tax payments, but again, nothing specific to individual properties. The real surge of excitement came when Tony read the tax returns prepared by the accountants and every piece of income was listed showing the source. There was definitely nothing for The Haven going back almost ten years. Some properties produced rent and then stopped before restarting, and one had been fire damaged producing an insurance payment. He had two final checks to make, but first another visit to the drawing room to return the documents. Upon entering he thought Miss Marchant was asleep, but she turned to hear him say,

'Just returning your documents and, if I may, can I go through the property portfolio with you to make sure I have everything?'

He proceeded to name all of the other properties he knew she now owned and she nodded as each was mentioned. She knew little of some of them and seemed confused by one or two. Eventually, she agreed that there were no other properties as far as she knew. He excused himself and then called upon Muriel Gamble and asked if she knew about the properties.

'No, I don't know anything about them, apart from Lizzie's, and I doubt anybody except the accountant will know anything as he is the only one she talks to. She doesn't even talk to him much.'

This seemed like success to Tony, a forgotten property and no way for it to be traced unless somebody in Cornwall still lived there and knew all about it - perhaps another mistress or her descendants. There was only one way to find out. When he arrived home, Jemma was waiting for him at the door.

'The children have been waiting for you all day; I hope this extra work is worth it,' she said. He picked Jemma up in his arms, kissed her full on the lips and said,

'Yes it is, my little angel; tell the kids we are going to have the whole weekend together next week. I've booked us a holiday cottage for a well-earned break.'

'Gosh, the whole weekend? Where are we going?'

'Cornwall.'

Chapter 11

He had indeed booked the cottage, about five miles from The Haven, and had taken the precaution of removing the deeds and any trace of the property from Miss Marchant's house. He had even found sets of keys in the vault at the Marchant house and noticed that four sets were not labelled. The unlabelled keys had not been touched for years but were now in his briefcase in the hope that one set was made in Cornwall.

On the following Friday he left work at lunchtime, and after changing at home, he and Jemma collected the children from school and set off on their long journey. It was late in the evening by the time they arrived at the cottage, having stopped for a meal on the way. In fact, both children and Jemma were asleep when he pulled into the drive of the holiday destination, courtesy of the satellite navigation system that had guided them. It had crossed Tony's mind to detour and try and find his main target property, but he decided he would leave that until tomorrow.

The children were up and out of bed early the next day and keen to adventure.

'Well, kids, you can either go to the water park or the bowling alley, but Daddy has to look at a site first so Mummy will take you for breakfast,' Tony announced to a sea of disappointed faces.

'Tony, I thought we were on holiday,' Jemma said through a frown.

'We are, we are, but I got a text about a possible deal and said I would have a quick look. I shouldn't have said where we were going; it's my fault.'

'Text from whom?' Jemma quizzed.

'It's a contact from a business club, but it might be good for us all in the end. It won't take long, I promise.'

He gave Jemma £50 and told her to take them somewhere nice in the village, which was a five-minute walk, and he would meet up with them later at the cottage. All of the rest of his time would be theirs. He was gone before Jemma could argue and drove away whilst entering the postcode for the approximate position of The Haven. He had positioned the address from a map and the description on the deeds and had looked it up on a postcode finder on the internet.

After a few minutes, the satellite navigation voice told him he had reached his destination, but he was confused. There was no property in sight, just the coast in the distance and rolling fields and hills. He drove a little further and came across a pub at the beginning of a very small village, which looked like it had been untouched by time. The pub was called The Scarecrow, and a very old painted sign of a scarecrow on top of a straw man swayed lightly in the breeze. As it was early morning, the pub was closed, but Tony knocked on the faded oak door. There was no answer, but an elderly lady was walking past and stopped beside him,

'No good knocking there, they don't live in the pub; they drive in just before opening time. It's never busy here until the school holidays.'

'I wonder if you can help me; I am looking for a place called The Haven.'

'The Haven?' she answered scrunching up her face.

'Can't say I know it; what does it look like?'

'I'm afraid I don't know, I just have the address.'

'There is an old place down Endercott Lane, but that's a few miles from here.'

'No, it's Nile Street.'

'Oh, Nile Street. That's mainly gone now because the developers have moved in. You are in the wrong place. You need to turn round and drive back along this road, and you will see a road on your right with a pile of new houses. That's where Nile Street used to be.'

Tony didn't know how to feel about the news. He had seen the new houses but assumed his postcode check was right. He turned the car around and drove back along the road before turning right into the area the lady had described. There was a sign to Heathcote Village. He passed a development of thirty or so properties and then saw a dirt track with trees either side of it. He took a moment to take in the scene, but there was no other road except the dirt track. There was nobody to ask, so he moved forward, turned down the track and drove for a few hundred yards until he came across a large, detached property standing in its own neglected grounds. The property looked Victorian or Edwardian with large bay windows at the front and two large black doors at the front entrance. There was no sign of life, but no vandal damage either. It looked like a smaller version of Helen Marchant's property in York.

Parking his car at the steps leading to the doors, he walked up and turned to the bay windows to look inside. The windows were ingrained with years of grime, but he was able to see inside the property which was furnished although most of the furniture was covered in dust sheets. He wandered around to the back of the property where he could see a very large kitchen hidden behind the almost grey glass windows, and again no sign of recent life. There were two outhouses which seemed to be used for vehicles, but no sign of a car or even recent tracks apart from his own footsteps. When he returned to the front of the house, he saw that there were some car tracks that suggested some sort of vehicle had approached the house in recent times, other than his, but it looked like it was not in the last few weeks. Time to try the keys. Heart now thumping, he tried the first two sets without success. There were three keys on the key ring of the third set, but he failed with the first two. The third key turned in the old lock, and he heard a click. Pushing against the door he found that nothing happened, and he thought he might be mistaken about the click but age, rust, and dirt were playing a part, and a more determined push caused one of the black doors to open with a noise like a creaking gate. The door opened about half way before sticking, and when he poked his head around, he saw a mountain of mail and free newspapers. Suddenly he felt nervous. What if somebody came now and asked who he was or took his number from his car and traced him back to Yorkshire. Whatever the apprehension, he pushed a little harder and he was in. As a precaution, he shut the door and took a second or two to compose himself.

Stepping over the pile of mail, he saw the high ceiling of the hallway and the cobwebs cascading from the chandelier in the centre. Four doors faced him in the rectangle of the hall, and all were closed. The first door he tried was to the room he saw from the window and appeared to be a drawing room or sitting room. It was clear that nobody had been sitting in it for years as the dust sheets were thick with the debris they had collected in protecting the furniture.

The furniture was antique or period and in fairly good condition. The brown leather chesterfield looked unmarked and unused as he peeked underneath its sheet. The next room was obviously the dining room, and a large mahogany table was encircled by 12 chairs. Something struck him as odd about both rooms, but he couldn't quite put his finger on it at the time. The third door took him into a small study, and when he removed the sheets, he saw a walnut writing desk, a captain's swivel chair and a large light brown leather armchair. The last door was into the kitchen which he had glimpsed from outside. The kitchen was almost like a film set of a period drama. There were kitchen cupboards rather than units and a large cooking range with copper pots and pans hanging from a wooden bracket, suspended by rope.

Once again, the dust was a major element in the room, but this time without dust sheets to catch it. Everywhere had that gritty texture of long-settled dirt and grime. It dawned on him what had seemed so strange in the other rooms as he checked out the kitchen. He quickly moved back into all three to be sure, and he was correct. There were no paintings or pictures on any of the walls or photographs on any of the furniture. Why?

He was calm now and trying to drink in as much information as possible. He did not dare stay too long as Jemma would be both curious and angry. An hour today to find out as much as possible.... The post mountain was the starting point. Having separated the free newspapers and leaflets, he created a pile of letters. Those that were obviously sales letters were thrown to the left, and there was still an enormous stack of others. Starting with the brown envelopes, he noticed that there were three different people named and they were Mrs Joanne Collins, Mr C. Armitage, and Mr Andrew Wilson. The letters dated from February 1984 to October 1994 and ranged from letters from suppliers of clothes, pet food, and wine to information from the council on development applications and road closures. Who were these people and where are they now? Why did all real communication stop in 1994, and was it really the case that nobody had lived here since 1984? The white envelopes were also, in the main, sales letters but there were two that were not. The first was handwritten, and was addressed to Mrs Collins and dated 16th of March, 1984.

Dear Mrs Collins,

We are sorry to have to write to you, but your account remains unpaid, and we cannot extend any further credit to you. George and I both appreciate how difficult things have been for you and do sympathise, but you must understand we have a business to run. I have tried telephoning you, but your line seems to have been disconnected so we would appreciate it if you would pop into the shop and sort matters out.

Yours sincerely,

Mildred Pertwee

The second letter really caught his attention. It was the only recent letter in that it was ten months ago and was hand delivered, as there was no stamp. The letter was on very expensive, thick paper and was from Carter Browne Developments Limited in London.

Dear House Owner,

We wrote to you a little over a year ago and do not appear to have received a reply. It may be that the property is subject to a trust or involved in some legal proceedings, but we would still welcome a discussion to see if there is something we can do to assist.

We look forward to hearing from you.
Yours faithfully,

Dominic Price
Chief Executive

A letter of almost a year before, so where was it? Tony frantically searched through the piles again to find another embossed envelope but could find nothing. Checking his watch, he saw that he had been there for an hour and a half and really had to wrap things up to come back later. He just couldn't tear himself away, and a final search of the envelopes, including opening the sales letters proved fruitless. Just as he was clearing up to go, he saw the stack of old free newspapers he had piled up and started his last search there. He unfolded each one, and after twenty or so, a letter dropped onto the floor at his feet. Unmistakable signature envelope, and his heart leapt as he grabbed it and pulled it open.

Dear House Owner,

As you will be aware, we have been carrying out significant developments in the area for the past few months. These developments have generally been well received and have improved amenities for local people, as well as creating much-needed homes and employment. We would be very interested in acquiring your property and would welcome a personal discussion with you, entirely without obligation. We should be most grateful if you would telephone the office and we can arrange to come and see you.

Yours faithfully,

Dominic Price
Chief Executive

Grabbing the letters he was taking with him, Tony closed the front door, locked it and drove off to catch up with his family. His head was spinning as he realised this was a huge opportunity for him and much bigger than anything else he was doing. This was the chance of a big hit, but he had to be careful. He had to discover what happened to the people named on the letters. He had to find out what their connections were to the Marchant family and how much the property developers would pay to own it. Another fork in the road; another hit of narcotic.

Chapter 12

Jemma had been irritated when he turned up, but his excitement had been infectious as they spent the day together, managing the water park and then ten pin bowling before stopping off at Pizza Hut for dinner. The kids could barely keep their eyes open as Jemma chatted away to Tony who smiled and nodded appropriately, but the whole time he was working on the information he had on The Haven and how he would use it. He even managed a second visit while the kids were getting ready for bed the following night. This time he went through the furniture to see if there were any other clues. Cupboards, dressers, kitchen drawers and bookcases all drew a blank.

The small writing desk had writing paper, envelopes, and stamps of some years ago, but little information on the occupier of the house. The bottom drawer on the left-hand side was locked; however, a sturdy knife from the kitchen took care of that. Inside the drawer were some bank statements, cheque books and, at last, some photographs. The bank statements were of two accounts, the first being Mrs J Collins and the second being Mr C Armitage and Mrs J Collins. The accounts seemed to cover 1974 to 1978 and had the usual expenditure attached to running a house. There were photographs of a man and woman together and also individual photos of them, 11 in total. In two of the photographs, they were joined by a teenage girl. Tony scooped up all of the contents of the drawer, placed them in a plastic bag, and was off back to his family.

He was now obsessed. Very little other than this small group of people entered his head on the long drive home. He had almost forgotten his other schemes until his mobile pinged with a text. Jemma picked up the phone and said,

'It's from Matthew Barker.' She then read it as Tony drove. 'Hello Old Man, hope you have had a nice break with the family. Don't forget we are at The Marsh House Care Home tomorrow at 11 am for the first of the surgeries. Cheerio'.

'Oh shit, I completely forgot,' Tony said, producing tutting from the kids in the back of the car.

'Sorry kids, text him back, Jemma, and tell him I will see him there.'

He had almost forgotten the scheme that he had come up with before the big fish had arrived. The plan involved seeing an effective captive audience in care homes to help them with wills and investments. Matthew hoped to pick up trust work and ultimately lucrative probate business when the clients died in what he described as God's waiting room. Tony's plan was worse, and that was to deprive them of some of their assets. In any event, his bosses were very keen on the idea and had supported it with leaflets as well as telling Tony he was free to spend as much time out of the office as he wished on these appointments. His appetite had reduced for the opportunities the care homes may present in the light of his major new target, but he had no option other than to go. Marsh House Care Home was not for the poor or indeed for the moderately well off. It was set in 16 acres of well-manicured gardens, and most of its residents did not need to worry about how to pay the enormous fees.

He arrived shortly before 11 am the next morning and met a somewhat bullish Matthew who shook his hand saying,

'Well, I hope we can pick up a few clients today as I've had our practice manager on my back again about targets and new clients. Apparently, if I produce a stream of clients, I get the brownie points for other work the firm picks up, even if I don't do it. The home has been on the blower to the office, and there are six appointments today, and at least two of them are loaded.'

Tony laughed and told Matthew he would do his best for him, although he was surprised they did not have their own professional advisors with all that money. The first appointment was disappointing in that poor old Mrs Herbert didn't know whether she still had a house or indeed if it was her house they were in. Polite general discussion followed with a promise to come back if she wanted any further discussion. A brief moment of interest arose when she said they may be better talking to her son Arnold about her money, but that interest was extinguished when the care home manager told them that Arnold had died ten years ago.

Matthew was really pleased with the second lady who had a substantial income and a house abroad. Tony was less interested upon hearing that her two daughters lived locally and one was married to a lawyer. It was the final appointment that raised Tony's interest and brought back his waning appetite.

'Mr and Mrs Burton live in one of our cottages and

want to talk to you about family trusts and investment income,' the manager introduced. Mrs Burton did most of the talking and explained that her husband had suffered a stroke almost a year ago which is why they had moved into a care facility. They had a house in Harrogate which was standing empty and two other investment properties which were let to private tenants. Mr Burton had been a senior manager with Shell UK and was on a huge pension. Mrs Burton explained that they wanted to set up a trust fund for their daughter and her two children, but it must exclude their son-in-law who they were sure was cheating on her. She must not know of this arrangement, however. They did have wills but wanted to change them, and they also wanted Tony to look at their investments. The family had been recommended to a financial advisor by their long-term solicitor and friend, but when they received bad advice, they had fallen out with the solicitor. Music to the ears of both Matthew and Tony. Tony, now fully charged, said,

'I think we can do a whole range of things for you, but I will need to make a fresh appointment as we will need quite a bit of time to go through things. However, I can already see that your deposit account with your bank is paying you a full 2% less than we can pay you as you helpfully brought that statement with you. I can arrange to transfer that across to us in the next few days and at least that is a good start.'

Once again that unerring instinct for prey had shown itself to Tony. Large amounts of capital and income, one child with a difficult husband, and reason for secrecy. Several possibilities had already occurred to him, but he would wait for his fact-find with Mrs Burton when he saw her on her own and then close in on the kill. The serving up of ready-made victims had, he reflected, made him hungry again for more, and the care home idea was perfect for it. There were three more visits to homes nearby in the next couple of weeks, and although they were not as affluent as the impeccable Marsh House, they still offered opportunity. In those days he still held the view that these were victimless crimes, if they were crimes at all, and that he was performing a sort of service that entitled him to a handsome reward. The picture of a predator lining up his helpless prey was one he fought hard to avoid.

He remembered that it was around the time of the care home visits that the dreams started; dreams that would cause him to shout out in the night and wake and alarm Jemma. When he didn't shout out, he would often wake covered in sweat. The bed would be damp and cold to the touch, and he would be wide-eyed and shivering in the dark. They were recurring dreams. One was of him being in a muddy quicksand and desperately trying to move his legs quickly, but every step drained him of his energy and moved him even more slowly. He would turn, and three large snarling dogs were walking over the mud, getting ever closer without hindrance. Their teeth were bared, and he could feel the imminence of their bite.

A worse dream was of him driving his car, with Jemma in the front seat and Anna and Toby in the back. Everyone would be laughing until it became dark; the headlights wouldn't work, and he couldn't see the road ahead. Instead of stopping, he continued at the same speed whilst peering out into the darkness. Then the car became airborne as it left the road amongst screaming, but he could not scream or warn his family. He would then be on the outside of the car, which was now in water, watching Anna and Toby pressing their faces against the rear window of the car as it sank into the river. They were screaming 'Daddy, Daddy', but he couldn't hear them, only see the mouthing of the words as the car disappeared. Try as he might he was unable to move his legs to get up and save them.

He also had one where a tramp talked to him, who introduced himself as God. He said he was watching Tony all of the time and would let him know if he needed to step in. The tramp followed him as he walked away and shouted after him 'Not everything is black and white. Look for the grey… look for the grey… YOU WILL RECOGNISE IT WHEN YOU SEE IT.'

All his dreams caused him to wake both startled and disturbed… but not for long. His path was now set, and reversing from that path did not seem an option. There was a momentum about the events of the day and a compulsion that would not be contained. He continued to enjoy the exercise of power and that he alone knew what was happening. His security was not sharing any information with anyone, including those closest to him. Whilst he gave thought to his approach to the new targets of Mr and Mrs Burton, he started to research the property in Cornwall, which was now at the centre of his immediate plans and, it seemed, tantalisingly within his grasp. Having finished his day at the office, he attended to the needs of his children, ate the evening meal with Jemma and waited for her to tire of the television programmes.

'I think that's it for me, Tony, I'm off to bed. Don't stay up too long yourself; you are beginning to look tired. Perhaps you are working too hard,' she said leaning forward and kissing him on his forehead.

'No, I won't be too long, just got a few things to catch up on for tomorrow. I will be on the laptop for an hour or so; you don't need to leave the light on.'

As soon as she had gone upstairs, he fired up his MacBook Pro and started his search. There was nothing on The Haven and nothing on the Marchant family, who seemed to have avoided any internet information. There was a lot on Carter Browne and their chief executive. A search of company information showed him they had assets of £86 million and last year they made a pre-tax profit of £10.8 million. Dominic Price was 46 years old, married (wife looked like a model), had three children, and they lived just outside of London in what seemed like an immense house that probably had live-in servants. All very interesting, but nothing compared to the planning link which showed outstanding planning applications and decisions. They had developments throughout the south of England, but the one that caught his eye was for a development for a site in Penzance for 36 detached dwellings, hotel, and small shopping area. The application had been strongly opposed by the locals, but by a small majority, the planning committee had approved it, subject to an access road and main services following a particular route. His temples were beginning to throb as he read on and realised that both the route and the road passed through the land upon which stood the house he had been in on his visit. He clearly was the first person to be inside of it for years. The final piece of information almost caused him to shout out with excitement. The planning permission was subject to the development starting within three years, and there was little more than one year left. He was sitting on a goldmine.

Chapter 13

He checked his watch. He had been working on his computer for three hours. He had to plug it into the mains to be able to use it as the battery was exhausted, but not so him. He now had a second wind and, having checked that Jemma was fast asleep, he worked on. Who were these people named on the envelopes? He tried a Google search for Andrew Wilson, but there were hundreds of them. He tried Mr C. Armitage, but there were thousands of Clives, Christophers, Colins and Charlies. All drew blanks when he added Penzance. He tried Joanne Collins and again achieved nothing. He was just about giving up and ready to join Jemma in bed when he tried one more search. The local paper seemed to be The Penzance Gazette, and he searched their website. They had an archive section which he tapped into, and again there was nothing with the search for Joanne Collins. Trying the house name, the other names, and even adding Marchant produced nothing. The first date he had seen on the letters was 1984, and it was reasonable to assume someone was living at the house up until that point. Going to the date search, he looked for stories from 1984 and flicked through them. After too many to recall, one caught his eye.

LOCAL WOMAN'S DEATH WAS SUICIDE
The Coroner's Court today found that the death of Mary J. Collins was suicide. Coroner, Maxwell Derbyshire, held that the evidence was clear in that although Mary Collins did not leave a note, she had been suffering from depression for some years and had

deliberately ended her life with an overdose of prescription drugs at her disposal. The Coroner added that the death of her young daughter Abigail last year in a motor car accident had clearly had a devastating effect upon her.

Was the J an initial for Joanne, and was this the woman on the envelope? What was her connection to the Marchant family and the other two people receiving mail at the house? Was the teenage girl in the photographs the girl who had died in the car accident, and was she the child of one of the two men named on the letters? There were no other details on the abbreviated piece in the archive, but he had something to go on. He went upstairs to bed and quietly undressed before moving in to Jemma's warm, slumbering body. He didn't sleep a wink all night, or what was left of it.

The next day, the mystery was all he could think about, although he worried that heavy investigation was dangerous as it may alert people as to his intentions or at the least create a trail back to him if things went wrong. It was, however, reckless just to take over the property and sell it, hoping that nobody was going to lay claim to it. He knew how to register a title at The Land Registry and even felt he would have no difficulty in tricking the self-imposed recluse Helen Marchant into signing documentation, but could he be sure that once he did, there would be no alarm bells ringing. He had two appointments in the afternoon but hardly paid any attention to the chatty customers and their investments, as his mind was elsewhere. Just before leaving that day his private line rang.

'Hello, Tony, old chap, are you free to speak?' said the somewhat excited Matthew Barker.

'Yes, of course.'

'Really hit the pay dirt with the care home thing. I have three sets of instructions on complicated trusts, several new wills, and several will revisions.'

'Do they all pay well?' Tony genuinely enquired, for no particular reason.

'The trusts always do, but the wills are loss leaders, so we get to do the probate when the old dears step off their mortal coil... and looking at some of them that won't be too long.'

What little respect Tony had for Matthew was slowly evaporating, and once again he was thinking that it was not fair that a dim wit like Matthew lived a life way above his own. This feeling was increased when Matthew added,

'I take it I can still count on your help in the completion of the probate work? You have such a head for figures and detail, and as you know, I don't. I will, of course, pay you for all the time involved. How are you getting on with that frightful Marchant woman?'

Tony confirmed things were going well, but he was spending a lot of time on collating everything and had some way to go yet.

'Don't worry about that, Tony, we have just sent her our latest whopping bill on account, and since she has never trusted anybody in her life before, she realises all of the information has to be found. She is scared about the family stuff going into the wrong hands, so she just has to put up with the intrusion and the expense,' he said with a chuckle.

'Oh, by the way, I have been to see Mr and Mrs Burton, and we are underway with them. She has taken a shine to you, Tony, you charmer you. She says she wants to do everything through you and even wants to give you Power of Attorney. I said that is normally a member of the family, but she said she couldn't do that and you would understand why.'

'Okay, Matthew, I will pop round to see them.'

When he got home that night, he spent some time with the kids, and when he came downstairs, he walked into the kitchen to hear Jemma ask him what he wanted for dinner and what sort of a day he had. He was answering in a monotone, uninterested way when Jemma looked up from the large open fridge and said,

'I forgot to tell you that I took a call for you earlier on… let me find my note.'

Jemma searched around the kitchen, still wearing the scars of the children's meals. Finally, when she moved a casserole dish, she said,

'Yes, here it is. A Muriel Gamble wants you to ring her when you can. This is her number here. She sounded a bit worried about something, and I said I would pass on the message when you got in this evening.'

Having explained to Jemma who the caller was, he said he would give her a call while Jemma continued with dinner.

'Hello, Muriel, Tony here. I gather you want to speak to me.'

'Oh thank you, Tony. It is alright if I call you Tony, isn't it?'

'Of course it is, Muriel. What's the problem?'

'It's Miss Marchant. She is in a foul mood and banging around the place. She says she can't find all her bank statements and says I must have moved them. Well, I don't look at the papers on the desks and tables, and I might have moved them to clean, but I wouldn't have moved them far.'

'She gave the papers and statements to me, Muriel, but I returned them to her when I saw her in the drawing room. She did get most of the stuff out of her desk originally, but I left before she returned them. Perhaps she put them somewhere else.'

'Oh, I bet she put them in the footstool when I came in and forgot that she did it. The old cow is terrified I might see something, but I wouldn't understand it if I did. I will have a look tonight when she goes to bed. Hey, don't you tell her I called her an old cow. I feel bad now.'

'Don't worry, Muriel, no fear of that. You and I are friends aren't we?'

'Well, I like to think so,' she said timidly.

'Tell you what, Muriel, I will pop round after work tomorrow and check that everything is alright.'

'You don't need to that on my account.'

'I know, but I want to. See you at about six.'

The following evening Tony drove up, and Muriel answered the door before he knocked and ushered him into the kitchen.

'You were right, Tony; she had hidden them statements from me when I had gone in, and they were there in the footstool. I saw them there, and when she went on again I said we would search together, and I made such a thing of going through the dresser, then the table drawers before I said "what about this stool?", opened it up and said "are these the things you are looking for?". Well, you should have seen her face... bright red she was... no apology though.'

Tony laughed, and agreed to a cup of tea as Miss Marchant was out for the day on a hospital visit and then out to a restaurant. Mr Gamble was picking her up around nine. It was safe to talk, and Tony raised the history of the house and Helen's father. Muriel was glad of the company and happy to talk about all of the gossip she had heard whilst working for the family.

'Muriel, you told me about Lizzie Edmondson and her house. Is it possible he had other women?'

'I imagine so, he was that way inclined, but I have never heard any other names mentioned. He did have a way of looking at women that made you feel uncomfortable. I never liked him, but I was very young when he died. I was just in my twenties then and was only working here part-time. He was always away on business. Never took Mrs Marchant with him. She was a lovely lady, very elegant and polite. They say she had money before she met him, but I don't know really.'

'Did you ever hear the name Joanne Collins? I saw that scribbled on a bit of paper in one of the files that I looked at.'

'Joanne Collins? No, I can't say that name rings any bells.'

Growing in confidence, he pulled out the pictures he had

taken from the property in Cornwall and told her they were found in one of the boxes in the vault on his previous visit. He showed her the picture of the woman he assumed was Joanne Collins.

'No, I have never seen her as far as I know.'
Muriel flicked through the photographs still shaking her head until she reached the one of the man and woman together.

'I've not seen her, but I am fairly sure that is Andrew Wilson.' She pointed to the man.
Trying hard to stop his pupils dilating and his voice rising, he replied,

'Who is Andrew Wilson then?'

'He was Mr Marchant's assistant. He used to organise all of his properties and travel arrangements and everything really.'

'What happened to him then?'

'Well, it was funny, he worked on for a few years after Mr Marchant died, then he left and moved out of the area. I have never heard any more about him. I always remembered him though because he tried it on with me once and I slapped his face. That's why I recognised him.'

'Have you heard the name Armitage?' he tried, as he felt he was on a winning run.

'Yes, that was Mr Marchant's name before he got married. He changed his name you see when he married his wife because Marchant was a better family. Posh people, eh? You can never understand them.'
Bingo.

Chapter 14

His mobile, switched to silent, buzzed again. 18 missed calls, last call at 8.03 am. He had been sitting at his desk since 7.15 am, and in less than an hour, the branch would be open. In less than half an hour, the staff would start to drift in and prepare for the day. He had a lot to get through in this trawl to his position today and was determined to remember it all and find the routes back to safety he had missed, the chances for a normal life he had spurned, and just how it had gone as far as it had.

The day he discovered that Mr Marchant had been using his previous name of Armitage had been a highlight. He knew he was on to something, and all of his instincts told him the massive prize was going to be his. Muriel had said that she had not seen anything of Andrew Wilson for many years as he had moved out of the area. Was he still alive? How could he find out more? Three more fruitless nights on the internet with Google searches on Andrew Wilson, A. Wilson, and every letter as an initial in front of Wilson produced nothing. Should he just assume he was safe and go ahead? Take the risk and have an escape plan? He could not bring himself to do it without some insurance in place, some information which guided him to the irreversible step of becoming the owner of someone else's property... of stealing it.

How he still hated that word and tried so very hard to disassociate himself from the description, however accurate it may be. More proof required.

The next day he searched his browser to find a private detective agency in Manchester. He discovered one offering complete confidentiality and discretion in the tracing of people, companies, and addresses. He rang Park Lane Investigations and asked to speak to an investigator.

'Hello, my name is Trevor Peters; how can I help you?'

'Oh, hello, my name is Patrick Baxter, and I am looking to trace someone who may be a beneficiary in a will,' Tony confidently presented.

'Yes, we can help with that, and we don't need to know why you need the information, Mr Baxter. What can you tell me about the person?'

'Not much I'm afraid. He is called Andrew Wilson, he worked for Bernard Marchant in York until the mid-80s, and then I think he may have settled in Cornwall. I can provide you with the Marchant address, but the family must not be contacted as he left in difficult circumstances, and I don't want them disturbed or upset in any way.'

'Do you have an address in Cornwall that he may have gone to?'

'Well, I have an address, but it's an old one.'

'That would help. Now so far as our work is concerned we can offer you a basic internet service where we have special skills at finding the right information that may not be available to the general public, or we can offer an investigator who will actually go to addresses and make physical enquiries,' he offered.

'How much are we talking about?'

'The internet service is £550 plus VAT, where we will do our very best, and the special service is £2,500 plus VAT, results guaranteed. If the man really existed, we will find him. Depends on how important it is to you.'

'We will go for the special service, please. I will transfer the funds to your account now if you can get back to me in a week.'

'In a week? Not sure we can do that,' Peters said, with a theatrical higher voice.

'How about if I pay a bonus of £500 on the result?'

'You watch too much television, Mr Baxter, but I will do it myself and try and get back to you in that time and will accept your bonus if I have done the job for you.'

'I thought you said results were guaranteed.'

'They are, but I can tell you are a serious man, Mr Baxter, and you will want a lot of detail. I will get it for you.'

They agreed that instructions would be given by email and so would the report. Tony agreed to transfer the basic fee that day, which he duly did. His two accounts were growing on a regular basis as some more of the planted seeds in wills and the completing processes of probate were bearing fruit. Two of the wills where he had slipped Patrick Baxter in as a beneficiary had borne fruit and, as expected, Matthew Barker hadn't spotted the recurring name. One Life invoices in a few more had also produced invoice payments that went unchallenged. The victims were all in the same boat; no obviously well-informed family members likely to look at anything other than their share of the estate. In the case of the three wills where Baxter was a beneficiary, the will-maker relied entirely upon Tony to approve the draft and signed in his presence. All three had been chosen carefully.

Tony now met Matthew at least once a month to go through the details of the work needed on new wills or the probate on those who had died. Tony would take home the probate files and prepare the statements of account for Matthew to approve and pass on for typing in the solicitor's office. No challenges had been forthcoming, and the money was coming in fairly regularly now, with more to come. Matthew had confided in him that he was unhappily married to Harriet, a wife chosen for him by an overbearing father as 'very good material', but she, like his father, seemed to have little respect for him. What little affection they shared had been extinguished with ten years of failed attempts at having a family. Matthew had even been surprised when the hospital results came back to show he had a normal sperm count, as his default position was it must be his fault. Tony was beginning to feel some sympathy for his stooge. It did not stop him using him as a feed for his frauds, but nothing compared to his Marchant chase and the chance of the perfect crime. Again, that word and the sting it produced. Perfect enterprise was better.

The night of the phone call, Tony drove home and, once he had parked his car, he walked to the door. As he moved to put his key in the lock the door opened, and there stood Jemma in a short red silk dress, open a little at the front displaying a glimpse of a black lace bra. Her hair was freshly cut and styled, and she was wearing bright red lipstick and full makeup.

'Hello, Mr Needham, I have a meal prepared. May I help you out of your jacket?' she said in a seductive soft voice.

'Help me out of my jacket? You can help me find my house! I appear to have turned up at the wrong address,' he answered, wide-eyed.

'Follow me,' Jemma signalled with her index finger and walked model style into the dining room, where the table was set for two, wine was poured, and music was playing.

'Erm... where are the kids?' he sheepishly enquired.

'With their Grandparents for the night; we won't be disturbed,' Jemma gushed.

The act continued, and Jemma served up Tony's favourite starter of avocado and prawns before the main course of belly pork which she had been preparing all day. A combination of the rich food, second bottle of wine, and Jemma's flesh on display caused Tony to grab her arm as she said she would clear away. It was a spontaneous act as he pulled her onto his knee. They struggled with each other's clothes until they made the bedroom and were totally lost in the moment.

The freedom of an empty house made their lovemaking loud and frenzied, and maybe for the first time in a long time, Tony's mind was free of planning and plotting as he was taken over by passion. Relaxing together in bed they both became a little self-conscious and giggly.

'Wow, can't say I was expecting that on a Thursday night,' Tony said, looking up at the ceiling.

'All part of the evening meal package,' Jemma said, snuggling in to him.

'Well, I can tell you it will get five stars from me on Trip Advisor, that's for sure!'

Tony felt Jemma laugh as her head rested on his chest, but he felt continued movement after the laugh and realised she was now crying.

'What's the matter, love?' he asked, as he pulled away and lifted her head towards him. That set off uncontrollable tears in Jemma who finally through the sobs managed to say,

'Are you seeing somebody else, Tony?'

'What? Why do you ask that?' he said, sitting up with a wide-eyed expression.

'You seem so different lately, as though you are here but not here. We haven't had sex in weeks as you are always away or late home or tired,' all interrupted by fresh tears.

Tony took hold of her sobbing face in both hands and looked deeply into her closing eyes.

'Look, Jemma, I am not seeing anybody else. I don't know where you think I would find the time, but even if I could I love you and I would never do anything to hurt you or the kids. I am very busy at the moment, and I am working on something to give us some real security and a better life. All the effort now will pay off, I promise. You just need to trust me.'

Jemma wiped her eyes and drew the bedclothes around her, suddenly self-conscious of being naked. She seemed reassured as Tony stroked back her hair and said,

'Hope you feel better now. What about dessert?'

'I thought you had just had that,' she said as she smiled.

The incident, when Tony recalled it, had done two things. Firstly, it made him realise that he was not behaving normally, despite his best efforts, and that was dangerous; secondly, he realised how much he did love Jemma and insisting that she trust him was somewhat ironic. She could never have guessed what he was really doing and how far he had gone. In many ways, it would have been easier if he was only seeing another woman as she might forgive that, whereas she could never forgive what he was doing, still less be a part of it. The thought of it brought him out in a deep, cold sweat as he heard her preparing the dessert downstairs. How could he get out of this mess?

All thoughts of this were forgotten when on Tuesday of the following week Tony was alone in his office, and the mobile of his alto ego Patrick Baxter vibrated on silent. His phone screen showed Park Lane Investigation, and he pressed the green button.

'Hello, it's Trevor Peters here. Is that Mr Baxter?'

'Yes, it is. How are you doing, Trevor?'

'Fine thanks. I have that report for you, Mr Baxter, and I think you will find I have earned that bonus.'

Chapter 15

Tony moved from his seat and flicked the Do Not Disturb sign on the door as he closed it. Returning to his seat, he picked up the phone.

'That's good news, Trevor. I'm sure you will email the full report, but perhaps you would outline it for me now, if you can?'

'Sure, how long have you got?'

'Give me the abridged version.'

'Okay, well it seems your Andrew Wilson was a bit of a character. He worked for Bernard Marchant from 1972 up until Marchant's death in 1977. Wilson was some sort of business manager. Marchant was into a wide range of things such as property, stocks and shares, and that kind of stuff, but he was being investigated for involvement with exporting arms to Africa.'

'What, handguns and rifles or something bigger?'

'The whole works apparently, including heavy artillery, but they never managed to prove anything. He was in with some aristocrat who wanted to put together a private army to topple one of the smaller African states.'

'Lord Garfield?'

'Hang on a minute let me flick through my notes. Yes, that's the chap. Anyway, the word is they were into a few things, and the Marchant guy was using some of his business connections and Garfield his political ones to make a shed full of cash.'

'And Andrew Wilson?'

'Well, the Wilson guy travelled a lot on business and

might have been setting up deals. He was a bit of a fixer, by all accounts, and made arrangements for his boss who was a bit of a player apparently, you know, with the ladies. So Marchant dies, and Wilson continues to work for the family, but it seems he helped himself to the family silver.'

'How do you mean?'

'He was investigated for misappropriation of funds, but no evidence was found.'

'Do you know what he was supposed to have stolen?'

'Money, or rather expenses, over a long period of time. You see that is what was interesting because his boss Marchant had a few secret accounts that the Wilson guy knew about, and when Marchant died, Wilson continued to live the high life on this money that the rest of the family really didn't know anything about.'

'Do we know what he spent it on?'

'No, but I spoke to the guy who did some of the investigating, long retired now, of course, and he said he remembered that there was some woman involved, and he thought she might have been a girlfriend of Marchant, but that Wilson was a second runner, if you get my meaning, and moved in as first horse when Marchant died.'

'Do we know where all of this happened?'

'No, Wilson or Marchant was very good at hiding their tracks, which might be because of where the money was coming from and keeping it all from Mrs Marchant.'

'So, they never found anything?'

'Not a sausage apparently, and the investigation closed down in the late 80s, according to my source.'

'Who is your source?'

'Can't tell you that now, can I? We have lots of serving coppers and ex-coppers up and down the country who are great for information on dodgy characters. Looks like your Andrew Wilson was one of them.'

'What happened to him then?'

'Went off to live in South Africa in the late 80s and married a local girl.'

'Is he still there?'

'His body is, he died in 2004.'

'Did he have any children?'

'None that we know of.'

'Well, that is very impressive, Trevor; you've done a great job. I will transfer your bonus now.'

'That's very good of you, Mr Baxter, and anytime you need anything else you give us a call. I will email the report across.'

It took Tony a few minutes to assimilate the news. He was disturbed by his next appointment: a young couple wanting a large mortgage on a small salary. He only half listened as he checked in and out of the story he had just heard.

'No, I am sorry the amount you would need to borrow is too great on that property. The maximum we could lend you is £160,000, and that would only buy you downstairs. You will have to find something in your price range or put the squeeze on your parents.' They looked shocked at this statement, and so was Tony, who was not normally so glib or patronising. Had Patrick Baxter taken over today? That night he nodded when Jemma spoke to him, talked to the children without listening to what they said, and watched a television programme where he could not have named a single person in it. When Jemma was asleep, he crept out of bed and sat in the darkened living room with a glass of brandy in his hand. Finally, all the rolling balls in his head fell neatly into their correct sockets, particularly when he read the detailed report.

Bernard Marchant was an illegal arms dealer who made secret money that he did not declare to his family or the Revenue as, of course, he was breaking the law anyway. Lord Garfield did take money, not for the honours list, but his part in the political smoothing of passage for the arms. He was probably involved as well. Andrew Wilson was in on the plots and schemes and was a well-paid fixer who knew where all the bodies were buried or, more importantly, where the illicit funds were kept. Marchant had bought The Haven in 1964 legitimately, but all of the running costs were paid from the dodgy accounts so that his wife never found out. Marchant moved one of his mistresses in, and she was having a separate affair with Wilson. When Marchant died, the expenses were paid by Wilson using those accounts. When Wilson was being investigated, the report confirmed that he was sacked and left the area. Did he move to Cornwall? The good thing was that a private investigator and presumably the police at the time had not traced Joanne Collins or the property in Cornwall.

Joanne Collins died in 1984, maybe because she was depressed about her daughter's death and anyway was living something of a double life with two dodgy men. Wilson sneaked off to South Africa thinking he was still being investigated. A little doubt crept in; why had he not tried to sell the property? Perhaps he didn't know where the deeds were or perhaps he did not know how to deceive the estate. Anyway, he didn't do it.

Helen Marchant had not seen the deeds and knew nothing of the property. The deeds were amongst a large pile of deeds, and you would have to know what you were looking for with old title deeds. The property was not registered with the Land Registry, and nobody had been able to trace the owner. You could bet that Carter Browne Developments had spent time and money trying to find the person who could sell them their priceless land. Mr C. Armitage was Bernard Marchant using his previous name. Here was the thing: there were only four people who knew about the history of the property or had used it – Bernard Marchant, Andrew Wilson, Joanne Collins, and Tony Needham. The other three were dead, and he had the keys, the deeds, and knowledge of its value. The trail was as cold as it could be, and the jackpot had been hit or was close to it. Now he had to get Helen Marchant to sign the necessary documents and take over the golden goose.

Chapter 16

Tony had always been confident that if he could have some insurance in place, he could complete the necessary documentation to become the registered owner of The Haven. His investigation had provided that insurance and he set up his next meeting with Helen Marchant armed with a pile of documents for her to sign, including the transfer of ownership deeds for the Land Registry.

He had researched the procedure and downloaded the forms, but when he spoke to Matthew Barker about the process of registering title, he began to have doubts. It would be easy enough to get a form signed, but would that be enough? Having set up the appointment, his ring on the doorbell was met by a whispering Muriel Gamble as she opened the door theatrically.

'Oh my God, Tony, you have caught her on a bad day. She was poorly last night, and we had to call the doctor out. He was going to have her admitted to the hospital, but she wouldn't hear of it. She eventually told the doctor to get out so she could get some rest.'

'Oh my word, Muriel, shall I come back another time?'

'No, she says she wants to get your visit over with, but you better be quick.'

Tony walked up the stairs to Helen Marchant's bedroom and on the third knock heard her faint voice asking him to come in.

'Ah, it's you, Mr Newman, they said you were coming, but I cannot imagine why.'

'It's Needham, Miss Marchant.'

'What?'

'My name is Needham.'

'That's what I said, isn't it? Can we get on?'

'I have some documents for you to sign. I have prepared more than I need so as to avoid bothering you.'

'You are bothering me.'

'Yes, I appreciate that, but I am trying to restrict the number of visits. These documents will allow me to schedule all of the shares information, savings accounts, other investments, jewellery evaluation, and some property stuff.'

'Bring them here,' she demanded. As he had imagined, she looked at the first two or three forms and then lost interest.

'Just show me where to sign them all,' she instructed, with a pained expression.

As instructed, Tony held each of twenty-two prepared forms with stickers showing where to sign and those that required more than one signature brought gasps of indignation. His heartbeat quickened as she reached the important document, but she simply signed where marked. He now felt in complete control.

Attention to detail was his forte. Simply having a document signed to transfer the property may not be enough. It might arouse suspicion and be refused by the Land Registry. It might also lead to some unwanted enquiry when he tried to sell. He had realised that the solution was to use two firms of solicitors to act for the respective seller and buyer and to be totally independent of each other. The trick was that he had to be the client for both firms. This was not a problem for his alias, Patrick Baxter, but he had agonised as to how he could instruct a firm to act on behalf of Helen Marchant. That is when he had his brainwave and played his masterstroke.

When authorising a new account at the branch, he had noticed he had a striking similarity on a photocopied passport to an Andrew Bains. It was not that they looked alike, but that Bains looked like an older version of him. In fact, one of the staff had made a joke about Bains being his real father. His genius was to photocopy the copy, but with a different address for Bains and rent a second property in Manchester for him as an address to match the passport. The document that Tony had arranged to be signed by Helen Marchant was a blank power of attorney, and when he left, he added the name of Andrew Bains as that attorney. A few days later he attended the offices of Marsh and Calder in Manchester and instructed them to act for him, or rather Helen Marchant, in the sale of The Haven. He had combed a little grey into his hair and wore spectacles to age him and be a closer match to the photograph. He explained to Pauline Ablett, a trainee solicitor, that dear old Auntie Helen was no longer able to get out and he was dealing with matters for her. The completed power of attorney, countersigned by the unwitting and careless Matthew Barker, was produced, and he was ready to go.

'So is Miss Marchant housebound?' asked Pauline.

'Yes, I am afraid she is and also very grouchy,' he smiled at the part truth.

'Well, the power of attorney appears to be in order. How quickly will you want the transaction to be completed?' she enquired.

'The property is empty, and I gather the purchaser is a cash buyer who wants to move very quickly as he has some plans for the property that are time sensitive.'

'Is there an estate agent involved?'

'No, the deal was done directly.'

'Very well, we will crack on. We will send a contract to the purchaser's solicitors, and then it is down to them how quickly they act.'

He provided details of the buyer, Patrick Baxter, and the solicitors appointed to act on his behalf and handed over the old title deeds. He also gave her the probate documents showing the death of Bernard Marchant and the details of the beneficiary and executor, Helen. The price of the property was £300,000. Two firms of solicitors then wrote to each other and started the process of a transaction where the same man was pretending to be two other people, Patrick Baxter and Andrew Bains. All mail was sent to his two addresses in Manchester.

Up until a week ago, Tony had wondered how he would pay the £300,000 even though he was effectively paying it to himself, but fate presented the solution. His two accounts where the misappropriated funds were kept had risen to just under £125,000 with more to come in the near future, but still well short of the cash he needed. He had thought of a variety of ways of doing it, one of which was putting through a bogus mortgage on the property and then repaying it, but all of the ideas were fraught with risk and created a trail back to him. His salvation came when his Patrick Baxter mobile rang, and he saw it was Georgina Pilkington.

'Hi, Georgina, Patrick here, how are you doing?'

'Oh very well, Patrick, and happy with the monthly return on my investment, thank you very much. Any chance of investing another £100,000 with you on the same deal?'

'That deal is closed, I'm afraid, Georgina, but I can look into another one if you wish?'

'That would be great, Patrick, and my best friend wants to come in as well. She has just got her divorce settlement, and when she has paid for her house, she will have about £250,000 left to invest. I told her about my deal with you, and she has been offered nothing as good anywhere else.'

'I'm not so sure, Georgina, as I don't have the time to meet any new clients.'

'Don't worry about that, Patrick, she is happy to go with my recommendation, and I told her that I haven't met you, but that you have a lovely voice. Maybe we can meet up for dinner some time,' she added, with a flirtatious giggle.

'You are a smooth talker, Georgina, let me make some enquiries and get back to you.'

'That would be great, Patrick; you are a darling.'

'No promises, Georgina, but I will try.' Problem solved.

That night as he drove into his garage at home he was bursting with excitement. He unlocked the door and swept

Anna up into his arms as he walked through the hallway into the kitchen.

'Right, my little princess, you can tell your brother and your Mummy that we are all going out on Saturday and we will eat anywhere you wish, play any games that you want to play, and Mummy can buy any new dress she wants.'
Anna squealed with delight as Toby ran through shouting 'ten-pin bowling, ten-pin bowling and McDonalds.' Jemma was checking the children's homework and looked across the kitchen table with a quizzical expression,

'What's all this about then, have we won the lottery?'
Tony put Anna down and lifted Jemma off her feet causing the children to squeal even more as their mother laughed and struggled with their father.

'Put me down you idiot; you are getting flour all over your suit.'

'Won the lottery? I won the lottery the day I met you,' he said, turning her in a full circle.

'Oh yuk, yuk, double yuk,' screamed the kids, laughing at their Dad's romantic attempts.

He was happy, so very happy. In that moment he was managing to combine Jekyll and Hyde into one character. Excited by his progress on his scheme, impressed by his own ability to create and complete a plan, and genuinely in love with his wife and children, the doubts, the darkness of his actions, and fear of the consequences of discovery were banished in the excitement of the moment. He felt alive, fearless, and in control. The darkness and doubts would return, but not for now.

Chapter 17

After the kids were put to bed, Jemma and Tony had dinner, with him still struggling to contain his excitement and drive to move onto the next part of the plan. He had no end game in sight and banished any thoughts of disaster or detection. He was too clever, he had built in too many escape routes, and there were few connections between him and his alter ego, Patrick Baxter. Jemma got up from the table and started to clear the plates. Tony got up to help when Jemma said,

'My Mum has been on the phone; she would like us over for dinner on Saturday night.'

'Saturday night? Oh no. I like to put my feet up and have a drink.'

'Well, you can do that at my parent's house, can't you?'

'Put my feet up on your Dad's sofa? I don't think so.'

'Why do you say that? He is always very nice to you; you know he is.'

'Yes, in that 'I wish my daughter had married a doctor or a lawyer' sort of way.'

'Don't say that, that's not true, he just wants his daughter to be happy. Why are you being so mean?'

'I'm not, but I bet he thinks you could have done better for yourself.'

'Oh, here we go, chip on both shoulders. You have this thing with your Dad, not mine. He has never said anything bad about you at all, and I'm sure my Mum fancies you.'

'All right, all right, I will go and be nice.'

For a second his mind went blank, and the images of the past left him as though he had tuned out of a TV channel. Tony, back in the chair in his office, glanced again at the clock on his wall which almost appeared to be moving in slow motion. He imagined it must be time for the branch to open, but it was only a few minutes since the last time he had looked. Still, plenty of time to continue this careful reconsideration of all of the things that had happened to him: all of the things that had led him to his current position. Ah, that current position... the reason why he kept going over events was to find some comfort. Where was that escape route he had missed? Maybe blame might be attached to somebody other than himself. The reflections of times past were mainly painful, but times with Jemma and the children brought a warmth, albeit temporary, as it was followed by a sense of dismay at how he had deceived them, let them down, and destroyed their innocence. He still searched for nuggets of good times, normality, and hopes of a better future he once had held. The warm feeling of a happy memory was a driving force in these reflections, but also that strange sense of achievement at his use of his intellect and the power he had exercised in his devious plans. He only needed the warmth at that moment and fell back into his thoughts of that day when Jemma mentioned dinner with her parents. He smiled to himself as he remembered that conversation and the dinner that followed.

Jemma's Dad, Robert Wainwright, had always been very friendly to Tony, and whilst Tony felt very guilty and embarrassed about getting his only daughter pregnant,

Robert had never complained or indeed mentioned it at all. When they announced their wedding plans he had only said,

'Congratulations, you know, Tony, that all Sally and I care about is Jemma's happiness, and we will support you wherever we can.'

What was it that made Tony uneasy about Robert? Why did he feel the need to check his own fingernails for dirt, his shoes for cleanliness, and censor all of his conversations for anything that might cause offence? Was it that he wanted Robert to like him, or was he afraid that he might not? Did both Robert and Sally harbour serious doubts about him? At the dinner, Tony had that familiar feeling of insecurity and inferiority whilst in the Wainwright's palatial house. This luxury was something Jemma was used to and something he could not at this stage provide for her. He wished he could dislike the Wainwrights and say they were driven by money and possessions, but they clearly were not. They were happily married and spent a lot of their time in community projects as well as being very good friends to a range of people from different backgrounds. Sally was a very attractive woman for her age and had managed to stay slim and modern in her dress. She was often taken for Jemma's older sister, to such an extent that Tony often addressed her as 'Sis' which always made her giggle and blush slightly.

He knew the problem was his, not theirs. If he was honest with himself, he was jealous of Jemma in that they were her parents and not his. The thought was uncomfortable for him, but he knew it well enough. Robert had an easy charm that his own father lacked, and Sally had a confidence and sophistication that his mother could never aspire to, as much as he loved his mother. He spent most of his time fighting this conclusion and trying to find faults in his parents-in-law that would lead him in a different direction and appreciate more the family that he had. Perhaps he was just a snob. Maybe it was as simple as that. Anyway, on the night of the dinner, the food was of the usual high standard, and Robert was on good form telling a series of anecdotes relating to his clients' property mishaps. The best one was a middle-aged couple who tried their hands at DIY and removed a supporting wall in the kitchen, which caused the ceiling to collapse around their ears whilst they were eating their dinner. Apparently, nobody moved from the table in the mayhem, and all looked at each other covered in dust and debris whilst still holding their knives and forks. It was at the end of the evening that Robert took Tony to one side when Jemma was internet shopping with Sally.

'Hey, Tony, I hope you don't mind me asking you something personal, do you?'

'Of course not, Robert, what is it?'

'Is everything all right with you two and the kids?' Robert asked, whilst looking uncomfortable.

'What do you mean?' Tony replied, trying not to sound startled.

'Well look, I am not supposed to say anything, but Sally reckons Jemma is on edge a lot lately, and the other night she seemed to be crying when they spoke on the phone. I mean, don't get me wrong I am not wanting to pry into your lives, but if there is a problem of any sort, we would like to see if we can help. By all means, tell me to mind my own business.'

Tony could feel a little heat emerging to his face and a small damp patch forming between his shoulder blades. Did they know anything? What might Jemma have said to her mother? Was he giving off signs of different behaviour, and most importantly was he arousing suspicion?

'Look, Robert, Jemma is your business. She is your daughter, and the kids are your grandchildren so I would never think you were intruding. I have been working hard lately and have been away a little more than usual, so maybe that is it. The kids can be a bit of a handful, and I try and get back to help out, but you know how it is sometimes. I just want to provide the best for them and think that if I put the effort in now, it will pay off in the future for us all. Maybe I've been overdoing it.'

Robert smiled and put his hand on Tony's shoulder,

'Oh, I know that feeling very well. When Jemma was tiny I had to work away quite a bit, and I missed them both, but sometimes you have to prioritise work. I know that's not easy.'

'I'll have a think and see if there's something I can do. I don't think this particular demand on my time will last too long, but I feel I have to go for it.' Tony replied.

'Of course you do, I know you are looking out for the four of you,' Robert added reassuringly.

'I'll have a word with Jemma when we get home and see how she is.'

'Oh, don't do that for God's sake, I'll get into trouble

for even mentioning it.'

'Okay, Robert, we'll keep this between us.'

'Enough said, son, just let us know if there ever is a problem.'

On the way home Tony mulled over the conversation and worried a little more about his father in law's concerns and perhaps his lack of belief in him. He felt that chip rising on his shoulder, but felt he had put Robert's mind at rest. In any event, he had developed the ability to compartmentalise all manner of things, so he filed that thought in a box and moved back to his big venture. He was sure he was on the verge of a life-changing deal that would give him lots of options. He had to stay focused on that and make sure he brought in the big fish, as well as being more careful than ever not to make mistakes. The first part was Georgina Pilkington, and that was his first call on Monday morning.

'Morning, Georgina, Patrick here. I hope I haven't got you out of bed.'

'Cheeky, I have been up for ages; well, ten minutes or so.'

'Well, good news, I can accommodate your further investment and your friend's, but there is an upfront fee of £2000, I'm afraid. The further good news is the return is 1% higher.'

'Wow, that is brilliant, Tony. I will ring Mandy now and tell her.'

'Mandy? That is your friend's name, yes? Can you text me all of her details and I will set up the account. Is she comfortable transferring into the company account directly?'

'Is that the same account I used?'

'Yes, it is.'

'Okay, then she will be happy to do that. I will text you her full name, address, and email details, and say you will be in touch.'

'Brilliant, Georgina, always a pleasure talking to you.'

Part one complete, or will be once the phone call is made to Mandy, the bogus certificate prepared, and the money transferred.

Part two, a call to Patrick Baxter's solicitors, Curran & Co, and a quick chat with Gordon Curran, a one-man band solicitor. He felt Curran was about 55 years old, but it was difficult to tell. He seemed to be the original jack of all trades whilst not quite mastering any of them.

'Hello, Mr Curran, Patrick Baxter here. I will be in a position to transfer the funds into your client's account in the next week or so and wondered if you could suggest an early completion date to the vendors.'

'Yes, I can do that but there is still some paperwork to be done you know, and I have some enquiries on the title of the property. I can't remember the last time I dealt with an unregistered title, so it is taking a little longer than usual.'

'I tell you what, Mr Curran, if you can persuade the vendors to complete in the next 14 days, I will be happy to pay you another £250 on top of your fee for the trouble.'

For a few seconds, there was silence on the other end of the phone.

'Mr Baxter, we are not bartering over a second-hand car here. This is a property of some significant value, and I have a duty to ensure that everything is as it should be.

Even if you didn't want me to do that I have a professional obligation, as well as insurers who would insist upon it.'

'I am really sorry, Mr Curran, I can see I have offended you, and that was certainly not my intention. I am just rather keen to move on as quickly as I can.'

'I will see what I can do. Good day to you.' That was a misjudgment on his part and an incorrect belief that some extra cash would be welcome.

Part three, a call to Pauline Ablett at Marsh and Calder.

'Hello, Pauline, Andrew Bains here. I gather the purchaser wants to complete quickly. Just to let you know that we are happy for that and I can drop the keys in at any time and sign the documents when they are ready. We are a bit worried about losing this buyer so do all you can to give him what he wants and complete as soon as you can.'

'They have not been in touch yet about completion, Mr Bains, but I will let you know as soon as I hear from them.'

All balls in play and just waiting for the result.

Ten days later he was at his desk going through the monthly figures with Melanie Forrester at the branch when Patrick Baxter's phone rang from his jacket pocket. His own mobile was on his desk in front of him, and Melanie looked at it, noticed it was not ringing, and then traced the ringtone to his jacket pocket. Tony immediately realised his mistake. He always had that phone on silent to avoid this very situation, and here he was with his assistant knowing he was carrying two mobile telephones. Their eyes met, and he realised she was suspicious, but she probably thought it was a telephone for another woman to ring him on. Whatever it was, he had to think fast.

'Is that your phone ringing, Melanie?'

'What, in your pocket?' she answered haughtily.

'My pocket?' Tony answered, making a fumbling pretence and looking in each jacket pocket.

'Shit, I must have picked up my mother's phone when I popped in to see them last night.'

The phone had stopped ringing, and Tony pretended to ring back.

'Hi Mum, was that you just now? Yeah, I know, I must have picked it up on the way out last night thinking it was mine. I'm really sorry, Mum, I will drop it in on the way home tonight. Just want to make a couple of calls to Australia before I do,' he then pretended there was mutual laughter.

'Sorry about that, Melanie, where were we?'

She looked like she didn't believe him, but any doubts would have been about another woman. When she left his office, he saw that the call was from Curran and Co.

'Hello, Mr Curran, Patrick Baxter here returning your call.'

'Ah yes, Mr Baxter, I rang to tell you we completed the transaction this morning and you are now the proud owner of... of... erm... just a moment, yes, here we are, the proud owner of The Haven in Cornwall.'

'Excellent, Mr Curran, thank you very much.'

'My pleasure. Oh, and by the way my fee note has been adjusted for the extra work in the sum of £250 plus VAT.'

Tony's hands began to sweat. There was no going back; it was all or nothing. Time to sell to a real buyer and hope all bases were covered. Was he going to be rich? Or was he going to prison?

Chapter 18

Even now, while reflecting on these events in his office from the dark psychological place he found himself, he still felt that excitement over the plan for the property and a sense of achievement at his cleverness in its execution. It was the only part of the story that still had the capacity to give him satisfaction and some warmth. He leaned back into the leather chair and remembered the step by step conclusion of the deal.

Once he had been told that the title had been registered at the Land Registry, he knew it was now in the public domain and hoped for contact by Carter Browne Developments. It would be so much better if they contacted him rather than the reverse, as it strengthened his hand in any negotiations. He had given himself four weeks from registration for their call, and if that did not produce anything, he would make a planning application on the property which was sure to alert Dominic Price.

It was shortly after the third week that Tony called at Patrick Baxter's Manchester address. He had called each week in the previous three to find circulars, free newspapers, and advertising flyers. On this day they were there again, but amongst them, he could see the familiar expensive embossed envelope that he had first seen at The Haven. His eyes widened as he bent to pick it up and a warmth swept through his body as he tingled with excitement. He took a moment just to hold the letter in his hand and prepare himself to drink in the information it would contain. He felt an inching towards the end game and ultimate prize. There was no tearing of the envelope; instead, his thumb gently pushed against the corner and slid along the expensive paper, carefully easing out the letter inside. He immediately saw the heading of Carter Browne and read very slowly and deliberately the contents.

Dear Mr Baxter,
Re: The Haven, Nile Street (now Heathcote Village), Penzance

I understand that you have recently acquired the above property and would very much like the opportunity of discussing your future plans regarding it. My company would be very interested in acquiring the property from you or entering into some agreement regarding some of the land. I have set out below my contact details, being my office and mobile numbers and my personal email address. I can be contacted at any time and am happy to come and see you at your convenience for a discussion.

I look forward to hearing from you.

Yours sincerely,

Dominic Price

Tony moved into the living room of the flat and sat down on one of the very basic chairs that were part of the rent. He read and re-read the letter before letting out a shout of delight and then punching the air as if he had scored a goal. He felt he had. Now was not the time to panic or grab. This had to be a composed and controlled part of the game. He would make Dominic wait and sweat over a reply. Dominic or his staff would no doubt be doing their research and may even knock on his door. He had anticipated this, and the possible surprise to Price that someone speculating £300,000 was renting a flat in a less than opulent part of Manchester. He also imagined that enquiries might be raised of Helen Marchant and the circumstances of her sale to him. He had covered both. Two anxious weeks later he called at the flat and there again was the trademark embossed envelope. Smiling to himself he tore open the envelope to read.

Dear Mr Baxter,

Re: The Haven, Nile Street (now Heathcote Village), Penzance

Further to my previous letter, I note that I have not heard from you and although I am anxious not to press you, I do have business in the North of England which brings me to your part of the country in the next two weeks. I think it may well be in our joint interests if we could meet so that I can outline some proposals to you. You are, of course, under no obligation to accept any proposals, but I imagine you would at least like to hear them. Please give me a ring on my personal mobile, the number of which is at the bottom of this letter and let me know if you are willing to meet.
Kind regards,

Dominic

Tony smiled to himself. It was now 'Dominic', not his full name, and he was giving his personal mobile number. His desperation was all too evident in the second letter, and the time-sensitive nature of acquisition was massively in Tony's favour. How much was the property worth?

Shortly afterwards Tony saw that there was a message on his Baxter phone from Pauline Ablett at Marsh and Calder asking his second alias, Andrew Bains, to give her a call. He was using the same telephone number for both and was beginning to wonder if that was wise.

'Hello, Pauline, Andrew Bains here. You left a message asking me to call.'

'Oh yes, Mr Bains, thank you for ringing. We have been contacted by a company wanting to speak to you about the property sold on behalf of Miss Marchant.'

'Really? Why is that and who are they?'

'It is a firm of solicitors in London who say they have a client who may have an interest in that property... just a second while I get the letter.' Tony could hear the shuffling of papers and the opening of filing cabinets as well as some low muttering before the telephone receiver was picked up. 'Yes, sorry about that, it is a letter from a firm called Marcus and Black in London, they are quite a big firm actually. Anyway, they don't say who their client is, but they say that they would like the opportunity to talk to Miss Marchant or you about the property we sold. They also mention that Miss Marchant's address does not appear to be correct. I really don't know what they mean by that.'

'This is very strange, Pauline. Do you have any idea

what they want?'

'None at all, but I can ask them if you like.'

'No, just give me their telephone number and the person dealing with it, and I will give them a call. Curious, isn't it? But it may be Helen's cousin, who has always been trouble, and if it is, Helen definitely wouldn't want to talk to him or let him have any details. I will get back to you if there is a problem.'

Once Pauline had provided the detail of the author of the letter, Tony realised he had to compose himself. He thought he knew who this was and why they were investigating. He had anticipated it, but he still felt a surge of anxiety driven adrenalin as well as discomfort in the pit of his stomach. His cover plan that he felt so watertight was now under review and seemed less invulnerable. He suddenly could feel a hundred different ways this could all go wrong as the doubts flooded in. The expectation of inquiry had turned out to be a completely different feeling to that of a real live enquiry. He needed to calm himself and think carefully.

He decided to go for a coffee and dropped in at the Radisson Blu Hotel in Manchester to find a table in a corner and order a cappuccino. He went over a variety of phantom conversations with this new law firm and realised that his hands were beginning to sweat. Things had seemed so straightforward when he had planned it, but could he be sure it was Dominic Price who had instructed them. Maybe it was someone who thought they had an interest in the property; maybe it was a relative of Andrew Wilson or Joanne Collins who had been alerted as to the ownership. Why had he not considered this before? If it was someone like that, it was possible that the police would become involved and would call upon Helen Marchant. He had put her address on the forms at another random unregistered property that he had come across quite by accident, just in case somebody turned up there, hoping to speak to her. That seemed such a good idea at the time but now seemed flimsy and capable of discovery. If the worst came to the worst, he would close down his Patrick Baxter identity, and since there was nothing to link back to him, he would be fine. Well, what if the police went to Helen Marchant with the sale of the property that she knew nothing about and the police interviewed him as the person who had access to the deeds? What if they took his picture and showed it to the two firms of solicitors who were dealing with Patrick Baxter and Andrew Bains? They would realise then. What had he done? His hands were now trembling, and he scanned the room as he felt he must be showing signs of distress and could even be under surveillance. He had to think rationally.

Once the coffee kick hit, he began to calm himself and think more clearly. The chance of any of his nightmares happening was small, and everything pointed to Dominic Price and his company. Intellect was wrestling with emotion in his head and intellect was beginning to win. When he was sure he could not be overheard in the hotel coffee bar, he telephoned David Smithson at Marcus and

Black. After holding at the request of reception for a few seconds, the line clicked,

'David Smithson here, how can I help?'

'Hello, Mr Smithson, Andrew Bains here. I gather from my solicitors that you have been in touch and would like to speak to me.'

'Oh, Mr Bains, you are the attorney for Helen Marchant, are you not?'

'Yes, I am.'

'Well, first of all, thank you for calling me. I realise this is a little unusual, but I have a client who has a special interest in the property Miss Marchant has just sold and would welcome the opportunity to speak to her if that is at all possible.'

'Speak to her about what?'

'It is a little commercially sensitive, but my client would be happy to meet with you for a confidential conversation and would be happy to pay any expenses involved.'

'Who is your client?'

'I'm afraid I cannot say at the moment, but if you would find out if Miss Marchant is at least prepared to speak with them, we can perhaps disclose it then.'

'I very much doubt that Miss Marchant would be interested in a discussion, especially when you cannot tell me who she is supposed to be talking to. Also, she is not well and needs to avoid any stress.'

'Oh, there would not be any stress involved. It is really about the background of the property,' Smithson replied, sounding a little defensive.

'I cannot see that is anybody else's business and this

all seems very strange,' answered Tony, now growing in confidence and being assertive.

'I can see that, but there is nothing to worry about. I can ask my client if I can disclose their identity, but I know they did not want to do that if Miss Marchant was not prepared to meet them.'

'I can ask her, but I am almost certain she would not be prepared to meet anyone, particularly in these circumstances.'

'Can you at least explain why the address we have for her appears empty?'

'Miss Marchant owns quite a lot of property and would not welcome someone snooping around her private affairs.'

'No, no, nobody was doing that, we simply found that letters were returned and upon enquiry were told the property was vacant. Please assure Miss Marchant we will not be disturbing her.'

'Very well, let me make some enquiries, and I will come back to you.'

As he put the phone back in front of him, he felt an anxiety gradually ease and his old confidence return. The reference to 'they' as a client implied a company, and the whole tone of the conversation suggested it must be the development company of Dominic Price. There was no outrage in the voice or indication of some sort of investigation. He was confident enough to make the next call. He dialled the number.

'Hello, this is Dominic Price's personal assistant, can I help you.'

'Oh, I'm sorry I thought this was his personal telephone number.'

'It is, but Mr Price is in a board meeting at the moment. Is there anything I can help you with?'

'My name is Patrick Baxter, and I believe Mr Price would like to speak to me.'

'Oh, just one moment, Mr Baxter, let me see if he will take this call.' Thirty seconds later...

'Mr Baxter, Dominic Price here. So glad you took the time to call.'

Chapter 19

His nerves had all disappeared now, and a steely determination and growing feeling of ascendancy had replaced them.

'Hello, Mr Price.'

'Dominic, please.'

'Okay, hello Dominic.'

'May I call you Patrick?'

'Of course.'

'Well, Patrick, you have recently acquired a property that we are interested in. Oh sorry, I said that in the letter I think. Anyway is it possible we can meet so that I can discuss some ideas with you which I think would be beneficial to both of us? I can arrange to come and see you or have you flown down here for a chat and be lavishly entertained by us,' Dominic said, with a laugh.

'Wow, you must be really keen, Dominic.'

'I suspect we are both men of the world and men of business, so I will not risk insulting you by pretending you do not have a valuable asset.'

'Thank you, Dominic, at least that rules out a wasted exchange and makes for a more sensible discussion.'

'I am in and out of the country quite a bit, but I am in Manchester next Tuesday if that is any good to you,' Tony added.

'Tuesday is fine, just name the time and place.'

'I tend to take a suite at the Radisson Blu on Peter Street if I am staying in Manchester so I suggest we meet there at midday, and I will have them lay on a light lunch. How does that sound?'

'Sounds absolutely perfect, Patrick. Very much looking forward to seeing you then.'

Tuesday could not come soon enough for Tony, but his plan was almost derailed by the detail of everyday life. Having booked an executive suite at the hotel for the following Tuesday, Tony drove back to Harrogate and arrived at mid-afternoon. He had overlooked the prospect of appointments on that Tuesday in his Tony Needham life, and upon returning saw that he was marked as out between 12 and three that day.

'Theresa,' he called through his open door, causing her to walk quickly to the opening.

'Why am I marked out next Tuesday?'

'You have a lunch meeting with the regional manager. It's been in the diary for a month or so.'

'Oh shit, I completely forgot. Can it be rearranged?'

'Well, you can tell him. He will probably hit the roof,' she replied.

He could easily rearrange Dominic; he just didn't want to. He was excited, and that meeting was his priority. He did make the call to Andrew Maxwell and invented a story about an opportunity he had come across for some mortgage business out of town, but the only day he was offered to meet this broker was the day of their lunch. Maxwell was a little huffy about it, but the prospect of more business won the day, and their lunch was rearranged.

When he got home, he told Jemma about being away on Tuesday.

'Tuesday next week?' she enquired, wide-eyed.

'Yes, is that a problem?'

'It is only your daughter's birthday, and we were taking her to the cinema and then to the ice cream parlour.'

'I completely forgot, Jemma, but I can't get out of it. We can do it on Wednesday instead, can't we?'

'What? Change her birthday? Oh, you are impossible,' she added, as she flounced off.

The entanglements of these different lives were beginning to catch up with him. He had a family and a full-time job as well as two aliases and a number of fingers in a number of pies. He had to manage to sidestep this problem and concentrate on the big pie.

On Tuesday morning he drove to Manchester and pulled into his designated parking spot at the hotel. He was shown to his suite which was perfect for him: a separate bedroom, an enormous separate bathroom, and a large sitting room with a table and six chairs. He arrived at around 10 am, and that gave him time to relax, have a coffee and gather his thoughts. In fact, he had too much time as he kept looking at his watch from 11 onwards as the time began to drag. At 11.55 am the room telephone rang, and the square illuminated on the phone showed it was reception calling. When he answered, the well-spoken female receptionist told him that two gentlemen were here to see him and he asked her to send them up. His hands were a little clammy, so he took out a hand towel from the bathroom and when the room bell sounded he dried his hands and threw the towel behind the armchair before opening the door.

'Patrick Baxter, I imagine, I am Dominic Price.' A right hand was extended by a tall, well built, slightly balding man in his mid-forties.

'Let me introduce Sean Appleyard, my finance director,' Dominic added, turning to the man standing behind him. He was shorter, a little overweight, and although well-dressed lacked the expensive style of his chief executive.

'Pleased to meet you both, shall we go inside?'

Tony showed them to the table, and there was the usual chit chat about the journey and the plans for the week. As Tony had anticipated, Dominic asked why he was staying in the hotel when he had a Manchester address. This was the opportunity to cover any visit that Dominic or his people may have made to his flat. He explained that as he did not really have a UK base, he needed a safe correspondence address, but he rarely stayed there. He told of a property he had in Amsterdam, a small place in Bordeaux, and otherwise a life of travelling around. Dominic seemed to accept the situation, and the groundwork was done. During his delivery of this totally convincing cover story, he even managed to surprise himself with his poise and assuredness. The clammy hands had dried, and any doubts about his ability to carry the day were gone. The time was now.

The Deal.

'So, Dominic, as we know, you have not come all this way for a pleasant conversation or to hear about where I live, so can we cut to the chase. What do you have in mind?' Tony delivered, whilst holding unblinking eye contact with Price.

'Very well, Patrick, as you may know, we have some developments in the area of your property and would like to buy it from you if we can agree a price acceptable to both of us. Do you have a figure in mind?' Price retorted, retaining non-threatening full eye contact.

'I wasn't thinking of selling at the moment, but I think you need to tell me what you are offering.' A moments silence as Dominic looked at his colleague, both nodded, and he answered,

'As I said, Patrick, I am a man of business and everything I see in you tells me that you are too. My board wanted me to negotiate up to £600,000, but I will go straight there and offer you that sum for the property. As you paid £300,000 for it, it would represent a 100% return in very quick time, which in anyone's book is very good business.'
The two men looked at each other for a couple of seconds trying to control expressions, give nothing away whilst trying to read each other. The short silence was broken by a knock at the door.

'That will be lunch, gentlemen. I hope you have an appetite as we may be here for a while,' Tony said, seizing control. He walked slowly to the door and let in two staff with trollies who set out lunch on the table of assorted sandwiches, salad, pastries, cakes, and tea and coffee. Bottles of expensive red and white wine were placed on the table with still and sparkling water.

Tony chatted to the waiters to extend the pregnant pause in the commercial conversation before giving each a

£10 note as they left.

'Looks very appetising, gentlemen, shall we eat and chat?' he said, as he took his seat at the head of the table. Dominic and Sean joined him and were as charming and composed as him. They were used to this type of environment and also used to getting their own way most of the time. Dominic was obviously a very smooth operator who looked like he was never fazed or panicked. The two property developers did not force the pace. Instead, they ate, drank, exchanged anecdotes, and gently probed their man as to what he did, how he came across his profit opportunities and in particular this one. Tony played the role of Patrick Baxter as well as any accomplished actor could have done. He talked of fictitious deals in the past and sidestepped the detail of this one. When carefully pressed again on how he acquired this property that they had coveted so long he said,

'We are in the middle of a negotiation, and I'm hardly likely to give any information away about my saleable asset, still less the background behind it. I imagine you would not be keen to tell me how you acquire your properties, would you?' delivered with a smile and received in the same way. The time had come, his rehearsed pitch assembled in his head, plates pushed to one side, and with a glass of red wine in hand, he moved on.

'So, this is the position as I understand it, but feel free to stop me if I am mistaken. You have a completed development near my property, but by far the most valuable aspect is the new development to the south-east of my property where you hope to build 36 very expensive houses, a shopping centre, and a hotel. Now, again I could be wrong, but the only way you can gain access to this development for services and a road is through The Haven, or at least it's land. Planning permission was reluctantly given, but if you do not start building in the next few months, it lapses, and is unlikely to be renewed. That would in itself be bad enough, but I understand there has been a change of councillors in that area where Labour now hold sway, and they would be against the development. Am I right?'

Dominic was showing all his sophistication and poise and maintaining his relaxed posture; Sean was less assured, and the smile had been replaced by a slightly open-mouthed stare. Tony's in-depth knowledge of the background of their development had obviously wrong-footed both men, and they could no longer think they were likely to get a bargain. Dominic leaned forward and said,

'Not totally accurate, but go on.'

'I believe I have what lawyers and developers refer to as a ransom strip and there are established ways of determining a value for those. I have done some research, and I gather the appropriate value is one-third of the increase in value of your site by having my property. I know you will be aware of that,' he said, followed by a moment's pause for effect and the offer of a top up of wine, which was accepted. Tony was surprised that his hand was so steady when pouring the wine.

'You may not want to tell me, but I can guess at the increase here because you cannot build without me. I am going to say the land has a nominal value or is worthless without me, but with access and services has a conservative value of £10 million upwards.'

Dominic managed a staged laugh, but Sean gave the game away by not joining in. Dominic responded,

'Large developments are complex beasts, Patrick; they rely on a whole host of imponderables and are fraught with risk. It is never easy to be accurate on costs or profit and to be certain of any return. I think you overestimate the value to us.'

'Do you want to take me through the figures, then, on the development? I will need to know any deal you have with any hotel chain and retail outlets for the shopping centre. In the development you did in Crawley, you announced on your own website the advance deal with the Hilton Hotels group and an agent for major retailers. I imagine you have done so again.'

The Price smile was beginning to fade, and he was taking on the appearance of a very accomplished, but cornered animal. Sean had long since given up any semblance of calm and was looking like a distinctly worried man.

'What exactly are you looking for, Patrick, you cannot seriously be asking for £3.3 million?'

'Remember, I am not asking for anything. I know, however, that some of your competitors would buy the plot to stop your scheme and build it nearby with the co-operation of the local authority. If they did that, your land really would be worthless. I have not yet spoken to them, but we could have an auction to establish the value.'

'My board would never agree to pay anything like £3.3 million, Patrick, and there is no site nearby with the same potential; otherwise we would buy it and just sit on the land.'

'Okay, Dominic, here is where we are. Time is against

you, and there is no easier route for development than your own land. I will accept £2 million to sell you the property.' There was another short pause where the two adversaries looked at each other. Price had stopped looking at or reacting to his financial director. Price shifted in his seat and leaning forward towards Tony said,

'What about £1 million? I think I can get that agreed by the board,' Dominic answered, without breaking stride.

'No, sorry, I have given you my figure, and the issue is what we can agree today, or we both make further enquiries,' was Tony's instant response.

Dominic turned to Sean and said, 'I think we need to make some calls and come up with our best and final offer.' Turning back to Tony, he suggested an adjournment for a couple of hours and then reconvening, which Tony accepted. The two men rose from their seats, checked their mobile phones and after a polite handshake left the room.

The time ticked by slowly, and Tony tried in vain to watch TV, but he constantly replayed the meeting and his control of it which made him feel like a victor against a very strong opponent. He also knew he had to keep up the performance level and not relax too much during this break. Tony's mobile rang and showed it was Dominic who asked if they could come back to the room. Tony said he would be happy to see them and would order some fresh coffee. It was a little over an hour since the adjournment and having settled back in, a less than relaxed Dominic pitched,

'Patrick, you drive a very hard bargain, and we simply cannot meet your demands, but we are trying to be creative here. What I am authorised to offer you is a deal which could be worth more than your figure, but is made up of cash, shares or share options, and possibly even a property abroad which would avoid UK taxes on your enormous profit.'

'Why would I want shares or options?'

'I shouldn't tell you this, but we are in merger talks with another large developer and the share prices are likely to go northwards in the very near future, especially if we can tidy up some loose ends.'

'Who is the other company?'

'I can't tell you that, Patrick.'

'Not interested then.'

'Blue Stone PLC,' Dominic said in desperation.

'Dominic!' Sean gasped.

'Look, Patrick, I shouldn't have told you, but we need to move,' Dominic said looking a little less comfortable that he had previously. Tony held his gaze for a second or two for dramatic effect before taking a deep staged breath and, leaning forward answered,

'Alright, final offer from me, £1.75 million cash. I am willing to sign a paper today agreeing not to discuss the matter with anyone else and to complete the sale in 14 days. You will transfer £100k of the money tomorrow into my account, and you can go ahead with your merger talks and your property deal. Last offer.'

'We simply can't do that, Patrick. You have to work with us, and we can come to a deal that might be even better for you.'

'Sorry, Dominic, but that is my final offer.'

'Well, I am very sorry to say we will have to leave it there.'

'That's fine, Dominic, it was a pleasure to meet you, and I wish you every success for the future.'

Tony walked them to the door and shook his very dry hand with two warm, clammy hands, as Dominic and Sean walked out. Two hours later Tony's mobile rang again, displaying Dominic Price as the caller.

'Hello, Dominic.'

'Hello, Patrick, you win. It's a deal.'

Chapter 20

Tony had planned to travel home that night, but his head was too full and the enjoyment too great to give up being Patrick Baxter tonight. At that moment he wanted to be Patrick Baxter forever, to have the properties abroad, and a reputation for being a successful businessman. To be rubbing shoulders with the elite, renting hotel suites, owning expensive cars, and living a high life. Above all, he wanted more of the taste of success that he felt then, the blood rush and almost sexual excitement of the chase and win. If he overlooked his criminal actions, he had discovered an ability to hold his nerve, to negotiate, to calculate situations, and to follow them through.

That evening he felt a narcotic high, and he wanted to keep it going for a little longer before he returned to boring Tony Needham. He telephoned Jemma and said he was staying at a Premier Inn as the day had gone on longer than he had planned, and he would come home after breakfast tomorrow. He spoke to Anna and wished her a happy birthday again, promising he would make it up to her and take her to Toyland in Harrogate and she could buy anything she wanted. She screamed with excitement, and he accepted the rebuke from Jemma.

He showered and then went to the hotel restaurant. He was still buzzing and ordered a bottle of chilled champagne as he looked at the menu. He ordered lobster with caviar dressing as his main course to suit his mood and status; he felt it was the least he deserved after his achievements of the day. The combination of the earlier wine in the room and the pre-dinner champagne made him a little heady and added to the general elation he was feeling. He was finding it hard to concentrate as his mind was filled with today's success and the possibilities offered by the money. Did he now have enough, or would he continue on with this new life?

At some point, he noticed an attractive blonde woman in her early thirties sitting three tables away and on her own. He thought he had seen her before in the hotel, but struggled to think when. Maybe it was when he had coffee last week or when he had popped in for lunch a couple of weeks before. She was checking messages on her mobile and wore dark-rimmed spectacles on the edge of her nose which highlighted her delicate, pretty face. She was wearing a dark grey jacket around a white shirt opened enough to subtly display a shapely chest. Her knee-length skirt had slightly risen up under the table as she had crossed her perfectly tanned legs whilst concentrating on her phone.

As the waiter approached her, she looked up and caught Tony's gaze. She was a woman obviously used to male attention, and she just looked away. Tony found her fascinating in his newly aroused state and also found that he kept looking at her, especially when he noticed the absence of a ring on the left hand. Although a little out of practice at this sort of thing, he was tempted to send over a drink but thought better of it. He also tried to clear his head a little. After an hour or so, she paid her bill and to his surprise walked over to his table.

'It's Mr Baxter, isn't it?'

'Yes, it is,' he replied, standing politely.

'I'm Stephanie Jennings from your bank.'

'Oh, of course, you are, I am so sorry I didn't recognise you. Well actually I did, but I thought I must have seen you at the hotel. I didn't place you at the bank.'

'No, that's all right. I didn't recognise you straight away, but I thought I would say hello.'

'Please, have a seat and join me for a drink.'

'No, I should be going really.'

'Oh please, stay for one drink, I have been on the phone or computer all day and haven't talked to anybody in the flesh,' he lied.

'Alright, one drink then.'

He poured the champagne and asked what brought her to the hotel. She explained that part of her job was evening meetings with clients, and she had just finished a meeting with two foreign investors who had offered to take her for dinner, but she made an excuse to end the evening and decided to eat in the hotel. He topped up her drink, and when the bottle was finished, she refused the offer of another bottle but agreed to a cocktail. She told him she was divorced, there were no children for her to worry about, and she hated going to clubs. She and her friend had tried internet dating, but she had ended up with a freak that kept sending her intimate pictures of himself, despite the fact that they had only had coffee together. She eventually called the police. He said that he was divorced and had been for a few years. He had never had children as his wife couldn't conceive and that had caused problems between them. He embellished the story he had given earlier to Dominic about his life and business and then told her of a fantastic deal he had done this very day in this very hotel. He pretended modesty in the story and suggested that anyone could have stumbled upon the deal. He told a story of seeing a property on his travels, tracing the owner, and buying it speculatively which lead to a big sale. This story made him feel he was getting the admiration he was seeking for his cleverness as well as sharing his success with an attractive woman. The conversation was light although his mood remained at a dangerously high level of ecstatic as they smiled at each other, exchanged anecdotes, and occasionally held a gaze for a little too long. He could not be sure how it happened, as this outlet for sharing the news of his success was all he was seeking, but somehow they ended up in his room, and then in his bed. Maybe it was the alcohol or maybe the adrenalin pulsing through his veins after the day's events, but here was a very attractive stranger in his bed.

The sex was uninhibited, and he almost felt like he had turned into Patrick Baxter. There was a surreal feel to the intimacy, the situation, and his mood. He felt no guilt until the next morning when he awoke to the enormity of what he had done. He had completed his betrayal of Jemma and the children, even doing it on the night of his daughter's birthday. There was now somebody else to consider, and another possible trace back to him. He tried to remember exactly what he had said and worried that the alcohol had robbed him of his normal caution.

When Stephanie awoke, he tried to appear untroubled and asked her what she would like for breakfast.

'I don't do breakfast, I'm afraid. I will just have a shower, and I will be off to work.' She slid out of the bed and walked naked past him into the bathroom. Even in his near panic, he was taken by her perfectly formed body, the confidence to flaunt it, and found himself staring until she closed the door. When she was dressed, she walked into the bedroom and looked into the mirror to put on her lipstick before turning to him.

'Well that was wonderful, Patrick, but I can see the panic on your face. Don't worry, I am a big girl and make my own decisions. You haven't started a relationship here. We probably had too much to drink, and both needed a bit of company, so you don't have to worry about me. I popped my number in your phone if you want to meet up again, but if you don't that's absolutely fine, and by way of proof, I haven't put your number in my phone.' She smiled a very confident smile as she spoke and then leaned forward, kissed him on the cheek, and was gone.

On the drive home, he could not stop obsessing about what had happened and the possible consequences of it. Every now and again he could feel his body temperature rise, heart rate increase, and perspiration all over his body. He must be composed when he saw Jemma. He telephoned the branch on his way and said it was a late meeting last night and he had stayed in Manchester but would be in as soon as he had showered at home. Jemma met him at the kitchen after he had let himself into the house.

'Oh, here he is, fresh from a night with his fancy woman!'

'What was that you said?'

'It has just been on the radio that travelling salesmen have, on average, three women in various places they visit regularly. You must have at least one in Manchester,' she laughed.

Was this a test? The laugh seemed genuine, but was she probing?

'Well, all I can say is travelling salesmen must have more stamina than building society managers because one woman is more than enough for me, thank you.'

As he walked past the mirror in the hall, he quickly looked at himself to see if there were any signs of stress or guilt that would lead to further enquiry. Satisfied that he was giving nothing away, he changed shirts after his shower and drove into work. Although only a short drive, he was intoxicated with thoughts and emotions. He had just pulled off a deal that had made him an instant millionaire, and it was largely untraceable. He had compromised himself with a new woman and betrayed his wife. Why had he done that? Despite that thought, he replayed the glances over dinner, the approach she had made to him, the laughing, the drinking, the sex, and that body... wow, that body.

Once into his office, he checked his schedule and had twenty minutes before his first appointment. Just enough time to speak to Dominic and cement the last remaining part of the deal and his security. Three rings on Dominic's phone.

'Morning, Patrick, hope you aren't ringing to gloat. If you ever fancy a job here feel free to ask.'

'That is very kind of you, Dominic, and I never gloat as it is bad for business. Anyway, you will make much more than me,' he answered, with a laugh.

'What can I do for you, Patrick?'

'A further condition of the deal, Dominic.'

'Surely you are not renegotiating, Patrick. There is no more money I promise you.'

'No, it's not the money. Assuming the transfer of the 100k today, we are locked in and will complete in 14 days as promised. It is about the enquiries you are making with the original owners which are irritating them. I have had Andrew Bains on the phone playing hell with me and suggesting I am behind it. We both know it is you.'

'What makes you say that?'

'I hope I may have established I am not an idiot, but I have had my people do some research and am happy with their findings,' he lied.

'Wow, you really are good; what do you need?'

'I will email a short draft to you, which if you sign it will be the last thing we need before completion, but I will read it to you now.'

Tony then read from the note in front of him the short script he had prepared which agreed that Dominic, his company, and anyone associated with them would make no further enquiry of Helen Marchant or anyone else concerning the property. In the event that they broke that agreement, there were hefty penalties. If Dominic agreed, then he thought the book was closed on the risk of discovery.

'That is a bit strong, Patrick, our legal department will have a fit.'

'Sorry, but I insist. You have started an enquiry which is mischievous at best, and only you can stop or restart it.'

'Okay, send it over and let me read it.'

'Will do, but remember time is against you not me.'

In mid-afternoon, Patrick's phone pinged with the signed document as an attachment to an email. Another major step to safety. That familiar warm glow of success pulsed around his body and was repeated at around 5 pm when he checked Baxter's account online and saw the deposit of £100,000. How he longed to celebrate again, to confide in someone about his skill and accomplishment, but above all he was having repeated flashes of his night with Stephanie and that body.

Chapter 21

The next few days were unremarkable as he settled into being Tony Needham again. There were no trips planned to Manchester and no other Baxter based projects to think about. He had the odd phone call to Baxter's solicitors to arrange the details on the sale of The Haven, but generally, he was performing the role of a building society manager. In fact, he had a very good week as several legitimate leads had turned into society business. Investment returns were high, and he found that his branch was in the running for an award on the level of new mortgage business introduced.

The following Monday he had his rearranged lunch with Andrew Maxwell, and he wondered why the regional manager wanted to see him in this kind of setting rather than the office. Had he been taking too much time away as his alter ego Baxter, and was he going to be asked to account for the time and the results? Had he claimed expenses, and had they been checked? In his preoccupation with Dominic Price, had he been careless elsewhere? Tony arrived at The Slug and Lettuce in Harrogate and to his dismay saw Maxwell already seated and looking at his iPad. Maxwell was perennially late, yet here he was early and appearing to be preparing something. A hundred images of potential trouble flashed through his mind as he approached the table.

'Andrew! Early and working, that can't be a good sign!'

'Oh, hello Tony, just catching up a little before the food.'

Tony sat down, and Andrew folded his iPad and placed it

on the table carefully.

'What would you like to drink, Tony? I was thinking of ordering just a small glass of wine as I am driving but, you can have what you like.'

'Small glass for me too, please. I like to stay awake for the afternoon appointments,' Tony said, with a confident smile.

They both ordered the wine and the food and proceeded with the normal chit chat about football and their respective sufferings supporting Leeds United and Sheffield Wednesday. After the starters had been cleared away, Andrew sat up straight and gave a look of now to business.

'How are you finding the job, Tony? Are you still enjoying it as much?'

This signalled a problem to Tony, and he tried to guess what was coming next whilst giving a bland reply about how time flies and there is never enough time to do everything, but he loved the challenges. All pretty standard corporate stuff as he awaited either the threat of bad news or the actual delivery of it. Maxwell fixed him with an unblinking stare and said,

'The thing is, Tony, that your branch is punching well above its weight. Investment is the highest in the group, and the mortgage business has increased by 40% in the last twelve months. Defaults on mortgages have, in the same period, gone down by 20%. The board is asking me how it is being done, and my only answer is we have a top man running it.'

A smile was breaking out on Maxwell's face as he finished the sentence, but Tony was still trying to take it in and guess what was to follow.

'Well, that is very nice of you, Andrew. I have a great team, and Melanie Forrester is brilliant with the defaulters. She almost becomes one of the family and finds a way out, short of repossession. Young Maureen Bradley has turned out to be a bit of a star and has managed to bully all of the members of her tennis club to change their mortgages to us. I just sit there conducting the orchestra.'

'You and I know, Tony, that any team has to be lead and if they are strong, it is because you have pulled it together. You see, the thing is I am moving up to board level in the next year or so, and we will be looking for a new regional manager. I can't say the job is yours as we have a process to follow, but I am sounding you out to make sure that if it was offered to you, you would accept.'

'Wow, Andrew, I was not expecting that. I hoped to move up one day, but I thought I would just have to be patient. I am really flattered, and of course I would say yes, if offered.'

The rest of the lunch was back to football and the latest thriller series on the BBC. Although he was sworn to secrecy, Tony rang Jemma, who squealed with delight. Here was good news he could share and feel the admiration that came with it. After that call, he felt a strong conflict with his two lives and for a while wished he had just imagined Patrick Baxter and his dark deeds.

That night he dreamt that he had been to dinner with Jemma, and on their way back to the car a man dressed all in black had stood in front of them demanding his wallet and his car keys. Terrifying as the figure was, Tony had leapt at him, and a violent struggle followed where the man lashed out with a knife and stabbed Jemma and then knelt on Tony's chest with the knife poised to strike, which had lead to him being awoken by his own scream. His subconscious was providing images to him of the conflicts he had created in his life. All such conflicts disappeared when Baxter's mobile phone rang late on Friday afternoon and showed the caller to be Curran & Co.

'Mr Baxter? I have Gordon Curran for you. Please hold the line.' After a few seconds, the call was put through.

'Hello, Mr Baxter, Gordon Curran here. I thought you might like to know that I completed your transaction about an hour ago, and we will arrange the transfer of funds into your account. I gather you received £100,000 directly and, having deducted our costs, I am transferring £1,646,150 to you.'

'Well, that is good news, thank you.'

'I do need to remind you, Mr Baxter, that you have made a considerable gain on this property which is taxable, but that is something you will need to discuss with your accountant.'

'Yes, I will do, thank you,' Tony said, whilst thinking that income tax evasion was the least of his problems. Patrick Baxter was not a UK taxpayer because he did not exist, and he may soon be disappearing altogether. A little while later he used his iPhone to access the account, and there was the payment staring back at him like some mountain that had been unattainable in a previous life but was now his. He checked both accounts, and his grand total now stood at just under £2,000,000. The reason it was not even higher was that he had done some research into Carter Browne Developments and Blue Stone PLC. Both companies were listed, and Carter Browne's share price stood at 49 pence, and their bigger rival stood at £1.22. Tony believed that the merger would now proceed because of the development that was possible due to his sale, so with that in mind he had bought a limited company called Matapac Limited and changed the name to Portcullis Investments Limited. He paid £200,000 into a new account he opened and bought £100,000 worth of shares in each of the two companies he believed would increase in value due to the deal he had done on the property. He could afford to lose the money if the worst came to the worst, but this was a new thrill seekers game in the world of big business and a chance to try something different.

He smiled to himself at the irony that he was using money he had stolen from the Marchant family to buy stocks and shares when Bernard Marchant had made so much money as a stockbroker. The word thief, even when thought rather than spoken, still made him wince, and he needed to play the details over and over in his mind to find an explanation that he could settle on. The Marchant family were unpleasant people who had probably acted badly to achieve what they had so that it was not an evil act to take from them... was it? This thought process was like a never-ending loop for Tony because as soon as he found some comfort in an explanation, his inquisitive mind immediately pulled it to pieces. The Marchant family may not be nice, kind people, but what about the delightful Mrs Brownlee? Or the very friendly and trusting Fiona Cummins? The faces and names of his victims began to stalk and harass him, and when exhausted by them he would fall into a fitful sleep where they took on more vivid images of damaged and desolate souls, often joined by his parents, his wife, children, and his friends. A price was starting to be paid.

The successful deal on the Marchant property had started him thinking of an exit plan, and a way back to his previous life but with riches in the background. The offer from Andrew Maxwell, or at least the promise of it, had encouraged him to believe that he could return to his career and his family, to pick up the threads of his former life if he could access the stolen money and come up with some explanation. He toyed with various plans and explanations of part-time property development with fictitious partners or stocks and shares speculations to justify the sudden growth in his financial position. He could even tell Maxwell that he had been doing it in his spare time as some form of clearing the decks explanation before his promotion. He smiled to himself on the stocks and shares part as he had checked in recent weeks, and the shares he had bought following his property sale had actually fallen in value. Exactly seven weeks after the deal was completed, he was flicking through the Financial Times in the branch when on page six he saw the headline 'Carter Browne Announce New Development'. He read on and saw that the Penzance development had been given a start date and that an amendment had been agreed with the council to add apartments on the site of The Haven. The article concluded that chief executive Dominic Price would not be drawn on rumours that his company was in merger talks.

Tony quickly checked the current share price of Carter Browne, which he had bought at 49 pence and had fallen to 42 pence the last time he checked. There it was today at 79 pence as he fumbled to find the calculator on his phone. He had just made £30,000. He may have been toying with the idea of an exit plan, but the uncomfortable truth was he was drawn to this life and had a thirst for it and all that went with it. Moments later he was on Patrick Baxter's phone, and after a few rings, it was answered.

'Hello stranger, I wasn't expecting a call from you.'

'Hi Stephanie, can I see you on Saturday? I'm in town overnight.'

Chapter 22

Tony shuddered in his office and wondered if the heating was working properly, or was the act of full recollection draining the heat from his body. The clock was now showing 8.25 am, and in 35 minutes the branch would be open, staff and customers would be living their normal lives and thinking about what was for dinner that night or what might be on TV; how he envied them. He rubbed his forehead as he struggled to remember where he had left off on his recollection train. Yes, that was it, the call to Stephanie.

His first task on Friday of that week was to explain to Jemma, or put more accurately, to lie to her so that he could cheat on her again. How little she deserved this deceit and how trusting she seemed to be as he said there was a complication on a property deal and he had to be away overnight. Anna had asked if she could come with her Daddy and stay in a real hotel. She promised she would be no trouble and would take pictures on her phone to help him and make sure he was not lonely or bored. What was left of the decent man he had been felt huge guilt and even shame at this innocent approach. Innocence, yes, that was what he was witnessing and reminding him of how much of it he had lost. Be that as it may, it did not stop him from driving to Manchester and booking a suite at the hotel. Nor did it stop his almost uncontrollable passion when he met Stephanie in the room. She had made an effort and looked even more attractive than when they were last together.

Their attraction to each other was obvious and did not now require the preamble of flirting or conversation. The restaurant booking was cancelled as they opted for room service and more time to expel several weeks of pent up lust for each other. Tony's head was spinning long before the second bottle of champagne as he felt almost out of control. Sitting in bed and eating the remnants of the room service food, Stephanie turned to him

'So, what took you so long to ring?'

'I suppose I have been busy, and I have been out of the country,' he lied, in that now familiar way.

'You just got back and thought you might like a shag then?' she laughed.

'It's not like that at all, Stephanie. I really don't know why I rang, other than I couldn't get you out of my head.'

'I told you, Patrick, you don't have to worry about me, but don't take me for granted either. I like you, but I don't want to be messed around. There is something different about you, and I might be in danger of falling for you. Please don't mess me around.'

'Don't worry, you seem too dangerous to mess around with.'

'You better believe it,' she answered, with another laugh.

As he drove home the next day, he felt like an alcoholic who had stayed off the booze for weeks but had just been on an all-night bender. He feared he would smell of Stephanie, or his eyes would betray him to Jemma. He knew what he was doing was wrong, but he did not want to stop. That was it. It wasn't that he couldn't stop, it was that he didn't want to stop, and that thought scared him. The Jekyll and Hyde elements were more in conflict now than ever before. He wanted both parts of his life but sensed that Hyde was destroying Jekyll or at the very least the life that Jekyll might enjoy. Upon returning home, he used his now consummate skill at role-playing to pacify his wife and children and control them with affection and reward. He was even developing a skill of suppressing the guilt and concern of discovery as he relaxed back into his family and professional life.

He settled into a daily routine of checking the share prices of his shareholdings. This seemed innocent fun compared to other parts of his life. A steady climb had started, but when the merger partner of Carter Browne was made public, the effect was dramatic. Carter Browne stood at £1.12, but Blue Stone PLC had shot up to £2.27, partly because the merger coincided with an announcement from them of further acquisitions and investments. His gain on the shares now stood at a whopping £172,000. He really believed he had discovered a gift within himself, a gift to outsmart the smart, to play the field on a wide range of issues, and to win. Having finished the share price search, he noticed that his Needham phone had three missed calls from Matthew Barker at Appleton, Townsend, and Palmer. He returned the call on the way into work.

'Thank you for ringing, Old Man. I am being chased by Mrs Burton, one of the ladies we saw weeks ago at one of the care homes. She says I was going to see her and set up a trust, but I think you were going to call and see them and find out what they had and how they wanted to set it up, weren't you?'

Tony struggled to remember the details in the vast filing cabinet in his head but recalled that he had transferred some funds to the society for them, and the mists began to clear.

'Oh My God, Matthew, I had completely forgotten what we agreed to do. Is she the wife of the guy who had the stroke?'

'Yes, that's her.'

'Shit, I'm really sorry, Matthew, I have had a lot on recently. I will give her a call today.'

'Good man, Tony, I am counting on you. Just send me the details and your fee note when you are done.'

Later that day Tony telephoned a slightly confused Mrs Burton to apologise for the delay and arranged an appointment to see her the next day. When he arrived, he was shown into their very smart bungalow, and Mrs Burton offered tea. As she went into the kitchen, he looked around at the furniture, which had obviously been brought from a much bigger and grander property. The antique mahogany dresser and table looked oddly out of place in this comfortable, but modern home. Attractive as it was, it was clearly nothing compared to their normal style of living. He looked around the room and settled on the silver-framed photographs of family events, including what appeared to be the Burton's wedding day. Here was a picture of two people much younger than him smiling with their whole lives ahead of them. Now he was going to be talking to an elderly lady who was a carer for the man in the photograph, who was unaware of the glittering career awaiting him when the picture was taken, but who could now not speak or remember who he was. After delivering the tea and biscuits, Mrs Burton went into another room and brought out a large box of documents.

'Well, here is everything I could find. I'm afraid my husband dealt with all of this, and I showed very little interest in it, which is bad, isn't it?'

'No, not at all. I tend to find that it is only ever one person in a couple who looks after the finances, and the other one just hopes that they are doing it well,' he said, soothing her discomfort.

Tony pulled out the documents, which reminded him of his much earlier visit to Theresa Mullin's Aunty Dorothy, but the difference here was one of scale. There were share certificates in various companies as well as investment bonds and offshore accounts. She even had the passbook for the North Yorkshire Building Society with the money he had transferred after their first visit. That feeling of searching for prey came over him, but he fought to resist it. He really didn't need to steal any more money or to take any further risks. He had far exceeded any plans that he might have had at the beginning and here was a chance just to be Tony Needham, the charming and likeable building society manager just helping out a nice old lady.

'Do all of these investments pay you an income, Mrs Burton?'

'I really don't know. Would you like to see the bank

statements?'

'Yes please.'

The bank statements were kept in a leather-bound folder, and Tony made notes of all income items. Some of the bonds paid income and some, particularly those offshore, just added the income to the total fund. One thing for sure was that the income they received was vast, and their current account accumulated much more than they spent.

'What I can do for you, Mrs Burton, is to make a list of everything, obtain valuations, and then you can discuss with Mr Barker the trust you want to set up.'

'Did I tell you that I don't want that son-in-law of ours to get anything at all or have access to any of it?'

'You did, but Mr Barker will take care of all of that for you.'

Tony made a list of all of the assets and said he would pop back to ask her to sign authorities to obtain the information, after which he would liaise with the lawyers. That night when the children were in bed, and Jemma was watching a property programme on TV, he settled down to look more closely at the investments. He made a list of the obvious ones that paid interest into the current account and were easily traceable and a separate list of those that seemed just capital based. He wondered why he was doing this as he had decided that he didn't need any more assets, as he called them to himself, to avoid calling it theft. Yet here he was still doing the preparation. One investment caught his eye in particular. It was an Investment Bond in the Cayman Islands in the name of Midland Bank Overseas Investments.

The Midland Bank had been taken over in 1992 by HSBC, but he could not see any new certificate. He had the Bond number and date of issue which was 18th October, 1979. Had the Burton's overlooked it?

Three days later, Tony popped into to see Mrs Burton with a pile of authorities he had printed out at home and went through the list of investments with her, leaving off the Midland Bond.

'Does that sound about right to you, Mrs Burton, or is there something else?'

'I really wouldn't know, but I gave you all of the documents I had, or should I say that my husband had.'

'How is he doing?'

'He is back in the hospital for further tests, as he was having trouble breathing the other night.'

'I am sorry to hear that as it must be a worrying time, but I will sort out all of this for you. At least I can do that.' All the authorities were in Mrs Burton's name as she was named on all the documents. Mr Burton had shared everything with his wife, which was just as well as he could not sign the forms. Tony had asked one further question which was how often they had moved house. The answer was quite a lot because of Mr Burton's career, which explained why the Midland Bond was still in place. Between 1988 and 1994 they had lived in South America so the letters from HSBC probably never arrived and the bond may well be lying dormant.

Two weeks later he received confirmation that the bond had indeed been placed into a Dormancy Account and that several letters back in the 90s had gone unanswered. The Bond was originally £5,000 and now had a value of £42,575. What should he do? He didn't need the money, but this was too good an opportunity to miss. Neither the tax authorities nor Mrs Burton would be aware of it, and he could discount any knowledge that Mr Burton may have had. The family dispute meant it was unlikely that anyone else would be involved. The Burton's had so much money that they would not miss this particular asset, and in any event, they would have to pay tax on it. He would be almost doing them a favour by relieving them of it. Another sleepless night followed as he wrestled with the permutations of action, risk, reward, and excitement. There was an outright winner the next day – greed. He prepared a document to transfer the proceeds of the Midland Bond into the account of One Life Investments Limited and had Mrs Burton sign it amongst several other forms he had prepared. She didn't even read it.

Tony delivered all of the valuations to Matthew Barker and his invoice for £1,800, which was paid directly into his account a week later. At breakfast the next morning he announced,

'Jemma, I have a nice surprise for you. I know I have neglected you and the kids with all this work, but I have just been paid £1,800, and it is yours to spend on anything you want.'

'Goodness, Tony, are you sure?' Jemma asked, looking excited at the unexpected windfall.

'Look, Jemma, I'm doing this for you and the kids and

you should enjoy it.'

Jemma pulled Tony's seat away from the table to sit astride him at the kitchen table and was about to take it further until the kids arrived, pulling their faces and making vomiting noises at their parent's passionate display.

'Okay, kids, that is enough. I was going to let you have some pocket money, but you can forget that now,' Jemma said, smiling.

'Oh, we didn't mean it, Mummy... how much?'

There was a lot of laughing, a lot of planning on the spending of the cash, and the house was filled with satisfaction and love. Jemma made good on her promised passion that night, but the problem for Tony was that during it, he was still having flashes of Stephanie.

Chapter 23

The Burton money arrived safely into the One Life account, and Stephanie's bank wrote to Patrick Baxter offering a range of financial services for the vast amount of money sitting in the accounts. Tony even spoke to his financial service friend to obtain general advice on investing large sums and started placing money in offshore accounts. These were all legitimate accounts, but with an eye to an exit plan. Tony had in mind that he must eventually have most of his ill-gotten gains in places where he could have access to the money away from the gaze of the Inland Revenue.

His information on how the accounts operated was helpful in understanding the process, but he then researched the offshore world and looked for places where the regulations were less onerous, and accounts could be opened in various names without the need for full proof of identity. If he was ever going to be pursued by the police, he was going to make it as difficult as possible to trace anything back to him. He opened three different accounts in the Cayman Islands and used the names of Patrick Baxter, One Life Limited, and Melanie Forrester from the branch. He felt really bad about Melanie as he had taken her passport identity from the staff file and opened it in her name. She would never find out, he reasoned to himself, and once he had internet access, he would be able to operate the account.

Having researched further on the internet, he opted for the Municipal Bank in the Cayman Islands as they had a reputation of not co-operating with tax authorities around the world. He would transfer funds into the One Life Account from the UK, and then once in the Caymans he would transfer them into the two other accounts and the money would be available to spend. If he had to close down One Life and Patrick Baxter, he would be able to use the Melanie Forrester account to access money and imagined that his bank would not disclose information to UK Authorities. All of this was done by telephone and on the internet. He was so careful that he bought a different laptop computer to use on these transactions so that there was no trace on his other devices. The laptop was kept in a small lock-up that he was now renting near his flat in Manchester. Separation of all things was vital to his plan of escape in the event of discovery of any of his dishonesty. There seemed little chance of that as he surveyed his new-found wealth from a position of security. He had been almost obsessed with caution in coming to the conclusion that it seemed increasingly unlikely that he would be caught. Was he any different to large financial institutions that took advantage of their customers? Or the Inland Revenue, who never gave overpaid tax back unless they were asked? He even had a plan for Jemma, to ease her into the expectation of large sums of money, and in so doing explain to her the need for him to be away more which would give him greater freedom to be with Stephanie.

He chose the Yorke Arms in the Nidderdale Valley to break his news to his wife and move on his plan. Jemma's parents had the kids, and he had booked the Michelin star restaurant and a room there for the night.

'Call it your birthday present, darling,' he told Jemma.

'My birthday isn't for three months, and I haven't got anything to wear that is good enough for that place,' she replied.

'Buy something then, but we are going, and I hope you enjoy it as I have mortgaged one of the kids.'

She did indeed buy something new and was very excited when they arrived, and they were shown to their room where a chilled bottle of champagne was waiting for them.

'Wow, champagne as well. Can we really afford all of this?' she enquired through a nervous smile.

'I will tell you over dinner, my impatient little one. Have a drink.'

They dressed for dinner and enjoyed a further drink and their starters, before Tony broached the subject.

'So, Jemma, do you remember I told you I was working on something, which is why I have been away a lot and that you had to trust me?'

'Yes, of course, I do.'

'Well, one of the deals has come off, and we are about to receive our first payment which is - wait for it - fifty grand.'

Jemma leaned back in her chair, wide-eyed but silent for a second. She looked down at the floor and then back at Tony.

'Fifty thousand pounds? Is this all legal?' she said, without thinking.

'What do you mean all legal?' Tony replied, with ironic indignation.

'I mean, you said I couldn't mention it to anyone, and now we are getting this big payout. I know you wouldn't do anything illegal, but Tony, it is so much money. I don't know what to say. What exactly do you have to do, and who are these people you are involved with?'

'They are not people you have met, but I was approached by a contact that I met and asked if I would be interested in working with a small group of business people on property developments. They had the cash, but didn't have knowledge of the mortgage market and wanted me to advise them and maybe eventually join them. I couldn't do that because I would have to leave the society, and my contract of employment prevents me from working part-time in any other job without their permission. I didn't ask permission as they would have said no, and this was too good an opportunity for us.'

'So, how did you get so much?'

'We did a development in the south, and I helped them raise money with a bank and then helped with marketing and setting up financial products in the sale, and the £50,000 is part of my share. There is more to come.'

'Wow, Tony, that is brilliant. Can we spend it, or do we have to hide it?'

He was pulling Jemma into a web of collusion, which was giving him the chance to draw some of this money and spend it with her, and at the same time win greater freedom from her to live his double life.

'We don't have to hide it, but we shouldn't flaunt it too much, as it will raise too many questions. When I am made up to regional manager, I will get permission to do some property deals on the side and just not mention I had done some already. We will be up and running then, and the sky is the limit for us.'

'God, Tony, I didn't realise you were so ambitious.' There was then a little pause and a slight change of atmosphere, which lead Tony to ask if there was a problem. Jemma thought for a second or two, then answered,

'I worry that you are changing and that we might not be enough for you anymore, you know, me and the kids. Maybe I have had a little too much to drink. I'm sorry, I should be happier about all of this,' Jemma said, sorrowfully.

'No, Jem, you have got this all wrong. You and the kids are my world. I am doing all of this so we can have the future we want. I want the kids to go to the best schools, have the best holidays. I want us to have better cars and buy what we want when we want it. Is that so bad?' He was losing confidence in his pitch, as the prospect of the money had not had the effect he expected. Jemma seemed to be thrown by his desire for the money and interpreted it as a lack of satisfaction with her and the children. In that moment, he wished he had been satisfied with the comfort of his family and their very good standard of life. Instead, he had rowed himself so far out to sea that he could think of nothing else other than to continue to row. The shore seemed too far away to go back. Jemma's eyes became moist, and she looked down at her glass of wine.

'We seemed to be happier a couple of years ago when you weren't working as hard and were home most of the time. Sometimes I look at you, and you are miles away. Sometimes in your sleep, you seem to be wrestling with monsters or chasing somebody or being chased. I don't know… perhaps it's me. I should be more ambitious, and God knows most women I know would love to have more money to spend after being stuck in with the kids screaming at each other all day.'

She smiled and seemed to be warming a little to the prospect of better things to come.

'Look, Jemma, I promise you this will all be worth it soon. I will be away a little more in the next few months, but after that, I will organise things better and be around a lot more.'

Despite the obvious discomfort of his wife, he couldn't seem to help himself winning more time away to spend with Stephanie and to the carefree life of Baxter. He felt some disgust at this manipulative lie about time away, but like so many other things in recent times, not enough disgust to stop doing it. The rest of the evening was spent drinking, flirting, amusing, and controlling Jemma so that she would accept his being away for the whole weekend in two weeks' time and for her to be discreet about his absence so as not to destroy his promotion prospects. He had pre-booked the hotel in London where he and Stephanie would spend their first weekend together, and he now had clearance to go.

One difficulty he had was that there must never be a traceable link between Patrick Baxter and him so that he could not just transfer money into his account. He had started withdrawing cash from Baxter's account on a daily basis from cash machines, using his £500 allowance and had withdrawn nearly £30,000 which he was adding to daily. Large sums of cash were supposed to be reported as suspicious transactions to the National Crime Agency. Tony had completed courses on this in his job, and the purpose was to stop money laundering for criminal use. He knew how the Agency worked and, in his view, things had to be mighty suspicious for any bells to ring. In his building society, they had a non-published figure of £5,000 cash, either in or out of an account, to trigger the report. He doubted that anything would happen with a report to the agency of a suspicious transaction, however, to be on the safe side he had opened an account for himself at Lloyds Bank and paid in different amounts of cash regularly as though he was paying in cash takings, but never more than £3,000 at a time. He could then transfer sums into their regular joint account without raising suspicion or causing a report. On the morning of his illicit weekend, he kissed Jemma goodbye and transferred £10,000 into the joint account telling her to buy whatever she liked for herself and the kids. In his car, he drove a mile or so and pulled over to use Patrick's mobile to text a message.

'On my way to the station, but a little delayed. Just meet me there at 12. Whole weekend to ourselves xx'
A few minutes later his phone pinged,

'Can't wait; hope you have plenty of stamina! xx'
A smile turned to a more worried frown as he wondered what he was getting himself into.....if he had only realised then, might things have turned out differently.

Chapter 24

*Oh What a Tangled Web We Weave When First We Practice
To Deceive.*

What a web indeed. Tony parked his car in Manchester
and rushed to the train station just in time to take up the
first class seats he had reserved. He had looked for Stephanie
on the platform, but there was no sign of her and nobody
in their seats. The train began to move slowly out of the
station, and he wondered for a second or two if she had
stood him up. After he had placed his case in the overhead
rack and settled into the window seat, the carriage doors
opened, and there she was carrying two glasses of wine.
She wore a cream trouser suit and a black silk shirt opened
enough to look sexy, but not too much to look slutty. Her
red lipstick was perfectly applied, and her hair was ruffled
as though she had casually run her fingers through it. She
smiled when she saw him, and most of the men in the
carriage looked up from their newspapers or laptops. He
felt a surge of pride and excitement as she swivelled into the
seat beside him, kissed him lightly on the lips, and handed
him a glass of wine.

'Thought we would start as we mean to go on,' she
whispered.
This was for him a dangerous game, but he not only couldn't
resist, he really didn't want to try. This was a fringe benefit
of his dual life and one that he was going to enjoy, even if
he did have to fight the image of his family life he had left
behind. The envious looks from the other men on the train

sustained his drive and suppressed his guilt.

The weekend was one of total indulgence in every way. Drinking wine at £100 a bottle, over ordering at restaurants, only to leave much of the food, and then drunken, wild sex back in the opulent hotel room. His head was spinning with the freedom to act as he pleased and spend the money he persuaded himself that he had won by his ingenuity. His one contact with his other life was his Needham mobile phone, which he kept on silent and inside his case. He would check for calls, especially from home, and would make calls to home when Stephanie was in the shower or asleep, when he would sneak out into the corridor or reception. On the last day, he saw that he had two missed calls from Jemma, and when Stephanie emerged from the shower he excused himself, telling her he was going to chat to the concierge about lunch reservations. Once in reception, he telephoned home,

'Hi, Jemma, missed a couple of calls when I was in a breakfast meeting. Is everything alright?'

'I think so, but I got a call from Matthew Barker asking if you could ring him urgently. He said he had lost your mobile number when he changed his phone and apologised for ringing on the home number.'

'Ringing on a Sunday? Did he say what it was about?'

'No, he didn't, but he sounded a bit stressed. I wasn't sure if I should give him your number so I said I would give you a call. I told him you were in London on business, and then I wondered if I should have told him that because of the secrecy thing.'

'Don't worry about it, love; it probably isn't a big deal as he is a bit of a fart. Anyway, I will call him now. What are you up to today?'

'We are going round to Mum and Dad's for lunch, and then to the cinema, I think. Dad says he has sorted something out for the kids. That normally means a film and ice cream until they are sick. What time are you back tonight? I have missed you.'

'I should be back about 8 or 9, but I will give you a call when I'm on my way.'

Why was Matthew Barker ringing? Why was it so urgent? It didn't sound good, but he couldn't think what it could be. Thoughts always turned to the Marchant family and something he may have missed, some piece of information which led to the discovery of the property in Penzance. Had somebody turned up asking questions?

'Hi, Matthew, Tony Needham here. I gather you have been trying to get hold of me.'

'Oh, Tony, thanks very much for ringing, and sorry to interrupt your weekend. Hope you aren't with your secretary,' Matthew tried to lighten his obvious stress.

'No, chance would be a fine thing. Anyway, she would eat me for breakfast. Is there a problem, Matthew?'

'Well, I hope not, but I got a call late on Friday from Mrs Burton. You know, that woman who wants to do the trust and has piles of cash.'

'Yes, I remember her, what did she want?'

'I saw her a couple of weeks ago and drafted something for the Trust and suggested she think it over and then see me. I set out a list of her assets and asked her to tell me what she wanted to go into the Trust document. Anyway, she rang me and said she had been talking to her husband and he got a bit agitated because there were some shares missing from the list and when they got the documents box out they couldn't find the certificate.'

Tony felt his temperature rise and his face flush as he computed this information.

'Hang on a minute. Did you say she talked to her husband? I thought he had suffered a major stroke. How would he play any part in all of this?'

'He did have a stroke, but it has only interfered with his speech and his walking. He understands what people say, and he can give instructions in his own way. I can't understand him, but his wife can.'

The body temperature climbed again as Tony realised he had made a huge mistake. He had never met Mr Burton and assumed the stroke was both permanent and totally debilitating. His enquiry of Mrs Burton as to her knowledge of their assets was now looking insufficient, and he had sold the shares and pocketed the money. There was no way he could put that back. Worse than that, this was a direct link to him. It was he who had gone to the house and he, not Patrick Baxter, that was the face to the client. Baxter was the receiver of stolen goods and a direct link back to him. That could lead to the discovery of everything else.

'So, Tony, is there any possibility that you missed something when you talked to Mrs Burton, because there isn't anything else on the list you gave me?'

'I suppose so, but do we know which company the

shares relate to?'

'No, that's the thing. Mr Burton can't write yet, but the hospital is teaching him. He apparently keeps pointing at the share certificates and is saying more, more, more. The reason I am in a bit of a panic is that I never got clearance from the managing partner to use you in these cases, and he will use any excuse to get rid of me. If the Burton woman makes a complaint, I am right in the shit.'

'I will go and see her when I get back, Matthew, and see what I can sort out. Don't worry about it.'

'Oh, you are a top man, Tony. The woman is acting like I have nicked their bloody shares. Do what you can, Old Man.'

When he ended the conversation, Tony slumped against the wall and closed his eyes. How could he have been so careless; how could he not have considered that Mr Burton would understand about his possessions? Why had he done it at all? He didn't need the money after all that he had achieved in the other cases, but he had succumbed to temptation and now faced discovery. Greed had undone him. He had to think and think fast. Gone was his desire for fun with Stephanie or even fear of Jemma's suspicion when he returned that evening. This was a potentially fatal mistake, which could lead to his arrest and all of his plans collapsing like a house of cards. Try as he might with Stephanie on the journey back, she had spotted the change of mood.

'What is it, Patrick? You have been edgy since you booked our lunch. Is it something I've done or said? It seemed to be going so well.'

'No, it isn't you, Stephanie. When I went downstairs, I got a business call which is a bit of a worry, that's all.'

'Why not tell me about it then and see if I can help,' she said, snuggling a little closer to him as the train gathered speed.

'I don't think I can tell you. Well, if I did tell you, tell you everything, then maybe you would feel differently about me.'

He surprised himself with what he said as he moved into a position to tell her something or even all of what he had been doing. In his anxious state, he even wondered if they could have a life together somewhere in the knowledge of his crimes. Would she support him or scream and call the police. His mind was rushing, his heart thumping, and his mouth drying as she replied,

'What makes you think you know how I feel about you?' she smiled and looked deeply into his eyes

'I didn't say I did know,' he said, playing for time to think.

'Well, Mr Baxter, I think I am falling for you like a giant redwood crashing to the ground. You have made me putty in your hands, waiting for a call as to when you will see me, and fitting me in between God knows what. Are you a spy or a gangster… or a drugs lord?' she laughed.

'No, none of those things, but I fly by the seat of my pants and cross lines that are perilous, and maybe a nice girl like you wouldn't like it.'

'Oh, you are making me hot, you teaser. Anyway, what makes you think I am a nice girl? I think I have established

I'm not,' she teased, placing her hand on his thigh.

He was tempted to unburden himself, but common sense kicked in. He would have to tell her he was married, that he had children, that he was leading a double life, and most importantly, he had been lying to her all along. Too dangerous.

'Maybe one day I will tell you everything, but not today, much as I am tempted.'

'Okay, your choice. I really don't mind what you do for a living or how you do it. I see all kinds of shady characters at the bank, and some of them have OBEs and CBEs, but would slice you up as soon as look at you.' She turned to look out of the window across on the other side of the train before turning back to him, 'Mind you, if I find out you are still married I will cut your balls off and feed them to you.'

Chapter 25

Jemma and the kids were delighted to see Tony, and he managed to stay distracted through the evening. Once in bed, he felt Jemma's body go limp as she fell into a safe, warm sleep with her husband back in bed beside her. How he wished he could follow suit, but he could not stop thinking of the Burton's and possible solutions. All of them seemed plausible until he reached the end and found a flaw that killed the idea stone dead. It was about 5 am when he finally fell into a fitful sleep filled with dreams of cliff edges, shark-infested waters, and death. The alarm clock woke him at 7.30 am into a day of destiny for him.

Once at the office, he cleared the early calls and telephoned Mrs Burton, but to his intense frustration there was no reply. He tried twice more in the next couple of hours before his mobile rang, and he recognised the Burton's number.

'Hello, Mrs Burton, I have been ringing you as I gather there is an issue about some share certificates.'

'There is, yes. My husband is adamant that he held shares in a company, and we cannot find the certificate anywhere,' she replied in a concerned, rather than hostile tone.

'Shall I pop round and see you both and see what we can do?'

'Yes, that would be very kind of you. My husband is really quite cross with me.'

'Will you both be in at around 5.30 pm today?'

'Yes, he has a hospital appointment at two, but we will be back by then. They see him on a Monday to help him with his writing. He is coming on very well. He still can't write a sentence yet although they say it is only a matter of time.'

'That sounds very encouraging,' he lied.

As he drove to the Marsh House Care Home, he considered his approach and how he would play things. He had rehearsed a dozen or so scenarios and rejected all of them before deciding to play it by ear and be reactive rather than proactive. He would feed off the Burtons and decide the strategy on the spot. He pulled up outside of their bungalow, took a deep breath, and walked to the door. The first point he noticed was that Mrs Burton was friendly and not suspicious of him upon greeting him at the door. He felt that was a good sign. They exchanged pleasantries and moved to the small living room where Tony caught his first glimpse of Graham Burton. He looked like a well-groomed man in his early seventies with no obvious sign of impediment. It was when he moved to get out of his chair that his mobility problem could be detected as he had difficulty with balance. He did stand unaided but had to steady himself on the back of the chair before moving forward and shaking Tony's hand very firmly.

'Hello, Mr Burton, it is a pleasure to meet you. I am here to try and sort out your affairs for the trust that you and your wife are setting up.'

Tony received a reply but could not decipher a single word of the response which was garbled, although Mr Burton seemed to present as though he thought he was speaking clearly. This was unlike listening to a person with a stammer who is very self-conscious and aware of the problem. On the contrary, it almost appeared that Mr Burton was unaware of the problem and expected to be understood. The very experienced ear of Mrs Burton was tuned in, however.

'He is saying that he is glad to meet you and hopes you can find his missing share certificate.'

'I wonder if we can start with any letters or documents you have to identify which company they were with. If we know that, then we should be able to obtain a duplicate certificate and then have them valued.'

Tony's heart was in his mouth as he waited for the translated response. If they knew the company, then it was going to be difficult, if not impossible to hide his theft, whereas if they did not remember the name he had options. Mrs Burton spoke to her husband who replied and again spoke to Tony.

'He says the shares were bought years ago when he worked abroad, and they were something to do with the seaside or the sea or something like that. I really didn't quite catch the last bit. You see, the stroke sometimes means he doesn't remember the right word.'

'Was it shore, or should I say offshore?' Tony didn't need a translation as Mr Burton nodded vigorously at the mention of offshore.

'What does that mean?' enquired Mrs Burton.

'Offshore just means the investment is held outside of the UK and does not attract UK tax unless it is brought back to the UK. The only thing is you should have been getting statements as to the value of the investments, and I didn't see any in the documents you gave me.'

'Oh dear, he is adamant we have them and says he did it through the bank.'

'Can you remember which bank it was that he used?' Tony enquired, knowing the answer but curious as to whether they did.

'He says it was The Midland Bank, but they have closed down now, haven't they?'

'Yes, they have, but we should still be able to make enquiries of the people who took the bank over.'

'We have been given the name of a very good solicitor, Mr Needham. Not Mr Barker, who I am sure is very good as well, but a solicitor a friend of ours used in some dispute they had a few years ago. He was like a tiger for them they said and even frightened them. Our friends said they were sure he will get to the bottom of it and find these shares if they exist. We had a disagreement with our previous solicitor, so we don't want to go back to him.'

A worrying development for Tony, and after a few minutes Mrs Burton offered to make some tea and Tony followed her into the kitchen.

'Look, Mrs Burton, you can, of course, instruct a firm of solicitors, but they will charge you £300 an hour to go searching for a needle in a haystack. You might find that the shares don't have a great value and you spend more in costs trying to trace them than they are actually worth. Let me make some enquiries for you, which I will do free of charge, as I should have checked with your husband in the first place. Just give me a couple of weeks.'

'That is very kind of you, Mr Needham.'

The tea made and delivered, Tony made small talk and after half an hour left a little easier. He had won a couple of weeks to organise something and, although a sword still hung over his head, he had an opportunity to escape as he had done before. He just needed to come up with a complete response that would satisfy the Burtons. What he had to avoid at all costs was anyone making an enquiry of HSBC who would confirm that shares in the name of Mr Burton were indeed traced and had been recently transferred to Patrick Baxter. Any hope he had was in avoiding any enquiry.

The next few days he found himself exhausted at the end of the day, but unable to manage any meaningful sleep. The tiredness would overwhelm him and cause him to nap in his armchair after dinner, only to be woken by Jemma gently tugging his sleeve. Once in bed, he would struggle to drift off and when he did he was easily awoken by Jemma's movement in bed or sounds from the children's rooms or downstairs. He knew that his next decision was crucial and thought of the permutations endlessly. Finally, he settled on a plan and nervously telephoned Mrs Burton to make a fresh appointment for the following day. When he arrived he was greeted by Mrs Burton at the front door, but as he moved into the house, she placed her hand on his left arm.

'I hope you don't mind, Mr Needham, but I have asked my daughter Karen to join us today, as I find all of this very stressful and frankly struggle sometimes to take it all in. Karen will understand it all better than me.'

Tony tried to hide his concern, which ran the risk of turning into panic. He was not very confident with the line he had decided to take, and that was before another party was involved. Presumably, this was the daughter with the husband who was to be excluded from the trust.

'Are we able to talk freely? I thought you told me that you did not want her husband in the trust. Will that not be a bit of a problem for you? You know, (lowering his voice to a whisper) talking about it.'

'No, Karen is my daughter from my first marriage, and we set up a different trust for her some years ago. Isabel is our other daughter or should I say my husband is her father. My husband has always been pretty close to Karen anyway, but she knows all about the problem with Isabel's husband.'

'So what does Karen do for a living then?' Tony tried to enquire lightly.

'She works for the police.'

Tony worried that his face had coloured with the news, and he also felt a trembling start in his legs as he moved to the living room door. Was this a setup? Did they already know what had happened, and were there other officers outside or on call? As he walked into the room, he saw Mr Burton in an armchair and Karen sitting with her legs crossed and looking a little stern. She was a woman in her late forties, slightly greying hair, and dressed in a formal skirt and jacket which seemed to be struggling with weight gained since they were purchased.

'Hello, you must be Karen,' Tony said, extending his hand.

'Karen Prentice, yes,' she answered, unsmiling, but at least shaking his hand, albeit from her sitting position. There was no warmth. Mrs Burton went off to make the tea, and Tony took the chance to test the water.

'As your mother is busy at the moment would you like me to answer any questions you might have, Karen... it's alright to call you Karen, isn't it?'

'I would like to know the background to what you have done so far, and what you are doing to trace these missing shares or bonds or whatever they are.'

There was no response to the question about using first names, and strangely Tony was offended by her tone. Whilst he had stolen the investments, she had no way of knowing that, and so far as she should know her stepfather had lost the certificate. The irritation he felt was because she should be grateful he was trying to help, but he could see the irony of taking offence. He had to stay focused and decide what he was going to do. He played for time.

'Well, in short, I think the problem is that Mr and Mrs Burton have not got any certificates or correspondence regarding these investments and cannot remember who they were invested with. I was given a box of documents and collated them as well as having values obtained, which is what I was asked to do. We have looked again at that box, and there was nothing else other than the items I collated.'

'Yes, but Mum says there is another one, and Dad is adamant that he arranged it when they lived abroad.'

It was interesting that she referred to him as Dad, which suggested a close relationship. He investigated further.

'Do you remember him mentioning it to you or your

sister, and is there anything to go on? Do you think there may be some bank statements, for example? There is no point asking the bank as they generally only keep statements for six years or so.'

'No, I am afraid I don't, nor does Mum. Do you think it is a waste of time?' There was a welcome softening of tone, which encouraged him to go on with his original idea.

'No, it isn't a waste of time, but I was anxious to avoid your parents wasting money on a possibly empty search. I have done some research based around the bank your parents were with, and I have a list of investments they were offering over a period of years. It is a question of sifting through them and seeing if we can come up with anything. I have called in a favour from an investment expert, who does not want to be formally involved for insurance reasons, but is helping me look,' Tony gathered confidence as Mrs Burton had joined them and smiled at the news of hope. It was she who responded.

'Oh, Mr Needham, that is so very kind of you. It is not the money you understand, but my husband is agitated by not being able to trace something he knows we had, aren't you Graham?' she said, patting his hand. Mr Burton smiled in response, which confirmed he was alert to the substance of the conversation. Again he felt a sense of his own carelessness and greed that he had put himself in this situation at all, but the route out was all he needed to concentrate on for now.

'So, Karen, what sort of police work do you do?' he enquired with a smile.

'Oh, I am a civilian with the North Yorkshire force. I am involved in administration rather than field work.'

With an internal sigh of relief, he felt that safety was within reach. He had an uncanny knack of getting himself out of tight situations. What a pity he kept putting himself in them.

Chapter 26

Once he had arrived at his office, his mood had lightened. He felt that now familiar feeling of being in control, of confidence in both the events occurring around him and his ability to control them. On the same day as his meeting with the Burtons, he saw he had a missed call from his father-in-law and wondered what that could be about. It was unusual to receive any calls from him directly as mostly they were on the landline at home and for Jemma or as part of some social arrangement. He returned the call.

'Hi, Tony, and thank you for returning my call,' said the ever polite and friendly Robert Wainwright. In fact, in that moment a deep feeling of envy flooded over Tony. What he felt then was a longing to be like Robert; respectable, successful in a totally honest way, and above all, trouble-free. One of those little snapshots in life that gives you an instant feeling of where you would like to be or who you would like to emulate in some way. It is not envy, but a momentary clear indication of where you may have gone wrong compared to the trouble-free life someone else appears to be living.

'No problem, Robert, what can I do for you?'

'I wondered if we could meet for a business chat? I know its short notice, but how are you fixed today? Maybe lunch?'

'Business chat? That sounds intriguing, Robert. I could do a working sandwich lunch here if you can make it, but I really can't leave the branch today as I have some catch up to do.'

'Sounds good to me, Tony, I will bring the sandwiches and the coffee. Can't drink that stuff you serve up there,' he said with a laugh.

Robert arrived at around 12.30 pm laden with wraps, deli sandwiches, Danish pastries, and two giant Costa coffees. They chatted for a while about family, social, and sporting issues whilst tucking into the food that would have served six or seven people. Eventually, Robert changed gear and said,

'Well, Tony, I have a proposition for you, which is why I wanted to see you. I haven't spoken to Sally or Jemma about this as I wanted to sound you out first.'
Tony shuffled in his seat and could not imagine what sort of proposition his father-in-law would have for him, but he invited him to go on.

'You see, Tony, I have for the last couple of years been discussing with some colleagues the possibility of property development as a separate business. I have done one or two smaller things myself, but my firm does not want to get involved in anything major. Two friends of mine have plenty of capital, but no expertise, and they keep badgering me to join them in commercial and residential projects. I can find these projects through work, but don't have the time to devote to them. One project has come up in the last couple of weeks which involves buying some land and building 25 houses on it. We are talking of setting up a company to do it and then looking for other opportunities. Would you be interested in being managing director?'

'Wow, Robert, that really is a lot to think about. I have

never thought about leaving here, and as Jemma will have told you, I am up for promotion in the next year.'

'Yes, I know, and I certainly would not want to put any pressure on you at all. What I have suggested to my friends is that you get involved with the first project unofficially to make sure it is something you would be comfortable doing, and then when the time is right, make the full time switch. The project is very profitable, Tony, and you would do very well out of it even if the first one was all you did. Then, if you moved into it full time, I would imagine you would treble your earnings here, or even better than that. I know these guys, and I trust them. There are plenty of opportunities out there for developing property.'

'Why me, Robert? Is it because I am your son-in-law?'

'No, absolutely not. In fact, it was one of my friends who mentioned you as he has dealt with you before and was very impressed. I shouldn't really say, but Jemma told her mum of your successful dabbling in property with other people, and that just confirmed to me that you were the right guy for this project. You know all about funding of domestic houses and your background in finance is perfect for us. Anyway, just think it over, and if you are interested, I will arrange a dinner so we can all get acquainted.'

'I certainly will think about it, and I am very flattered that you think I am the right man for the job, Robert. I am just a little taken by surprise, but if you trust these guys, then that's good enough for me on that score.'

'Look, Tony, there is no doubt in my mind that you are the right man. I think you could do most things if you put your mind to it. In addition, Sally and I have come to think of you as a son, not just a son-in-law… you know that.' Robert's eyes began to moisten at this emotional confession and created a lump in Tony's throat as he so wished he was deserving of this very decent man's affection.

Here was another development which played totally into his hands. He could work for a year or so at both jobs and then move into a prestigious position where large sums of money would not be out of place. He could gradually bring his ill-gotten gains into his life without arousing suspicion with his own family and the wider world. Nobody need ever know if he could cover his tracks. In time, he would be entirely free of concern about discovery and all that went with that. He had been in a long dark tunnel which had given him the narcotic of excitement and danger but appeared to have no end to it. Now he could see the pinprick of light at the end of that tunnel and a way out into sunlight and safety. He needed to tidy up all of his dealings and review everything in a meticulous way. He could, after all, get away with his crimes. Just maybe he could have the penny and the bun.

That night he shared his news with Jemma, who burst into tears at her father's offer and faith in her husband. She was delighted and desperate for Tony to accept the offer. Tony said he needed to work things out in his study, and such was Jemma's excitement that she almost escorted him up there, promised no interruption from the children and as much coffee as he could drink. She kissed him on the head as he sat down and almost skipped out of the room. Tony took out a piece of paper and listed the things he needed to do.

Burtons: he had a plan which had risk, but if successful would end their interest in the missing investment and stop an investigation of him.

Georgina Pilkington and her friend Mandy: He had taken £400,000 from them and was paying them interest, but it was dangerous to continue, especially his original plan to steal some or all of it. He had made so much money he could afford to repay their money and would not repeat the error of greed with the Burton money.

All of the other victims were either dead or unlikely to be alerted. He was happy that Helen Marchant knew nothing of the property he had stolen, and Dominic Price was very unlikely to risk his business development with further enquiry, even if he was prepared to break the agreement he had entered into to keep everything confidential. Surely the Marchant property deal was safe.

He stared at the list for a few minutes, and the pinprick of light at the end of the tunnel grew into a full-blown escape hatch. The thought of Dominic Price reminded Tony he had not checked on his share investments for a while, and he charged up his laptop to do so. Whilst he was waiting he thought of the need to close down Patrick Baxter and to remove all of his assets. He had almost completed the transfer of funds to the Caymans, and he would give notice to the landlords on his rented property. He would close down his telephone and credit card accounts as well as his bank account. The thought of closure of the bank account was followed by the image of Stephanie and his need to end that relationship. He was reluctant to do it as he was drawn to her physically and now emotionally. He was always excited at the prospect of seeing her, and she made him feel vibrant, sophisticated, and alive, as if all of his senses were alert and working to their full capacity. Despite this, he knew they could not continue.

The laptop sprang to life, and he moved to the financial page he had been using. He looked for and found his two stocks, but blinked several times as he thought he might have the wrong page on screen or be looking at the wrong stock. He checked Baxter's mobile phone to get the exact names of the two sets of stock. Here it was on the phone:

BLUE STONE PLC purchased at £1.12 per share.
Shares purchased 89,285.
CARTER BROWNE shares purchased at 49p.
Shares purchased 204,081.

Right those were the correct names from the phone. He pressed 'w' to refresh the laptop page.
BLUE STONE PLC trading at £3.89
CARTER BROWNE trading at £1.94

Yes, that is correct at today's date. He moved to two different websites for share information to be absolutely sure and confirmed the same information. He quickly moved to the calculator on his phone, but his hands were shaking so much that his fingers kept pressing the wrong numbers. Eventually, he calmed himself to do it correctly and wrote the calculator numbers on the piece of paper in front of him, below the list of things to do. He sat back and stared at his handwriting without blinking for what seemed an eternity. There were his holdings and their value staring back at him.

BLUE STONE PLC shares 89,285.
Today's value £347,319
CARTER BROWNE shares 204,081.
Today's value £395,918
TOTAL £743,237
PROFIT £543,237

Tony could scarcely take it in. The thefts had been so calculating and time-consuming that he had lived through each moment as if they were military operations, but this was different. This was a whim, and if you ignored the possible argument of insider dealing on shares, it was completely legitimate. Here was all the money and more to repay those he needed to pay and to keep the fortune he had. He felt a surge of happiness which was more to do with the light at the end of that long tunnel of his and the belief that he was beginning to dare to have that he would find his way back to his family. There was the very real prospect of the security of an honest life from now on. He was also wealthy and could afford to buy things he could not have afforded before. At that moment it all felt worth it.

As the memories of that exhilarating day faded and he found himself back to today in his chair, he almost wanted to relive it again to feel that pleasure that washed over him on that day. What he knew, of course, was that feeling was not going to last.

Chapter 27

As he was sitting, lost in this reminiscence, he must have drifted off into a light sleep. He was so tired, so very tired, that the warmth of the central heating gradually warming him up, plus his lack of rest, had a soporific effect and his eyelids had lost their battle to stay open. He was not sure how long he had been asleep, but the sound of the front door to the branch opening awoke him. He heard stiletto-heeled footsteps and imagined it must be Melanie Forrester. She was normally the first to arrive and open up the branch, but today he wondered if she would come into his office when she realised the burglar alarm was not on. Maybe not, as she might just realise that he had arrived first. He looked again at the clock, which now showed 8.50 am. So he had ten minutes to finish this retrospective journey to the present moment, to his lethargic state of mind, exhausted body, and pounding head. Where was he? Ah yes, the moment of most hope, when the share values provided part of the route map to his escape.

It started pretty well, he recalled. He played his card with the Burton family and decided to do so by phone so that his face could not betray him if things started to go wrong.

'Hello, Mrs Burton, Tony Needham here. I think I may have some good news for you about the missing shares.'

'Oh, that is wonderful, Mr Needham, have you found them?'

'Well not exactly, but I have made significant progress.

With the help of my colleague, we have traced what appears to be something in your husband's name that used to be with Midland Bank. As you know, the Midland ceased to trade, and it looks like the new owners gave up looking for you when they could not trace where you were living. If this is the investment we are looking for it was placed into a dormancy account.'

'What is that?'

'I suppose it is where they put money that nobody is claiming and maybe they eventually keep it, but the point is that if it is your husband's investment we can get it back, or at least its value.'

'Should I ask my husband if he wants to just have the shares back or the cash value?'

'No, that is the thing. We can only have the money, and I think there is some embarrassment here because they want a confidentiality agreement if they pay.'

'What does that mean?'

'It means you agree not to discuss it with anyone or make any further enquiry.'

'Is that normal?'

'Yes, I would say so in these circumstances. Anyway, they have not yet confirmed that it is what we are looking for, and there are a lot of questions we have to answer first.'

'Well, we will be guided by you, Mr Needham, you have been so kind to us, and I know my husband will be very relieved that you have found them. Did they have much value?'

'Yes they did, we think it may be just under £40, 000,' he answered and amazed himself that despite his strong pang of guilt, he still was lying as to value to try and keep some of the money. He quickly dismissed the thought and asked a number of questions to carry on the pretence of satisfying the bank as to the bona fides of the claim.

After the call, he decided it had gone well, and he would give it a few days before ringing and confirming the good news of a result. He would concoct some documentation for the Burtons to sign and transfer the money into their account, and then he would remind them of the importance of the confidentiality clause and how aggressive banks could be if such a clause was broken. That should give him extra comfort and once again he would have skillfully escaped detection. His next move was the sale of the Carter Browne and Blue Stone shares and the huge influx of cash into his company, Portcullis Limited. He decided this was a clean company, and he would keep the money there. In fact, he would pay corporation tax on it and remain legitimate since there was unlikely to be any investigation into it. Even if there was, he had taken the precaution of paying the £200,000 from his offshore accounts rather than directly from Baxter's or One Life's accounts. There was no forensic trail back to the tainted accounts unless the bank in the Caymans co-operated, and he was sure they would not. The next task was more difficult than he had expected. He rang Georgina Pilkington.

'Hi, Georgina, Patrick Baxter here. How are you doing?'

'Sorry, Patrick, that didn't sound like you, but your name came up on my phone.'

He realised in his haste he had forgotten that he changed his accent when talking to Georgina, as she, of course, knew him personally as Tony Needham, her building society manager. As Patrick to her, he adopted a slightly more privately educated and deeper voice, nothing too dramatic but different from his own voice. He had overlooked this and silently cursed himself for his carelessness.

'Yes, sorry, Georgina, I have had a bit of a cold recently, but I am now on the mend,' he said adjusting his voice.

'What can I do for you, Patrick? Hope you haven't lost my money.'

'No, but that is why I am ringing you. There are all kinds of rumours about the bonds you are in, and I think we need to get out. I can sell them today and recover all of the money, but I need to act fast. Obviously, that goes for Mandy too.'

'Wow, I wasn't expecting that. The payments have been coming in every month, and it looked really good.'

'Yes, I know, but as they say investments can go down as well as up, and the word is that they may be in trouble. There is a chance that if I sell quickly, we may even get a premium of a few grand profit, but I need to move now. I will give Mandy a ring, and you can both perhaps think about it overnight and make a decision tomorrow. How does that sound?'

'It sounds okay, Patrick, but I really don't know what to do. I suppose I just have to trust you, don't I?'

'I think I have done alright so far. You have had some good income and if you get your money back and a little bonus then that is a good thing, isn't it?'

'Okay, will you be able to re-invest into something else?'

'Probably not, as I am taking a job abroad, but I will put you in touch with somebody who will be able to help, or you could talk to that guy from the building society… what was his name… Tony Norris.'

'Needham. Tony Needham at the North Yorkshire Building Society.'

'Yes, that's the guy. Anyway, let's do this first.'

The telephone call to Mandy followed a similar path and when he phoned both the next day they agreed to his suggestion of sale. He played along with the ruse for a while by subsequent calls before telling them both that he had secured a sale and a 6% profit on the sale which meant that Georgina would get an extra £9,000 and Mandy would receive £15,000. He felt he could afford to be generous and also reasoned that someone who had received a bonus was unlikely to enquire further. He arranged payments through his One Life account, after transferring funds back from the Caymans. That was one task complete, or so he thought until Georgina rang a week after the funds had been transferred.

'Hi, Patrick, sorry to trouble you.'

'Never trouble to talk to you, Georgina. Were you happy with your bonus?' he said referring to her extra £9,000 and then waiting to bask in her praise and admiration for him.

'Yes, that was great thanks, Patrick, you are a star, and I wish you were going to continue to guide me. Is there any chance you can do it from wherever you are going to be living? I thought the internet meant it didn't matter where you lived.'

'No, I'm sorry, Georgina, I just won't be doing that kind of work, I'm afraid.'

'Well that is a real pity, Patrick, but thank you very much for what you have done.'

'My pleasure, is there anything else I could do for you?'

'Oh yes, sorry. The reason I rang was that my accountant said he tried to find the bonds and the company on Google, but couldn't find anything. He just wanted to have it all correct for the tax return. Can you help?'

Tony was amazed, as he never imagined Georgina having an accountant and declaring her income. He had judged this particular book by its cover and may regret it. Thinking whilst talking, he said,

'He won't find anything on the internet as it goes through third parties and is not advertised. Who is your accountant?'

'Peter Connolly of Talbot and Son, he is a friend really.'

'Are they a big firm?'

'No, there are only two of them, and Peter is hoping to go part-time.'

Tony felt an immediate sense of relief that it was not a firm with great resources and therefore one more likely to accept what he said.

'I will send over a statement which shows the interest, and that should be enough for the Inland Revenue.'

'That would be great, Patrick, thanks,' was the answer, and another bullet was dodged. He felt like that cabaret act where a man starts spinning plates on sticks and eventually is frantically running from stick to stick to keep them spinning. Just as he stops one from falling another begins to collapse, and he is running again. Could he keep them spinning a little longer? And then, as in the act, collect all the plates and take a bow?

Tony allowed himself the luxury of relaxing a little and ran through his exit plans once again. He concluded the Burton deal and arranged for both Mr and Mrs Burton to sign the document he created before transferring £40,750 into their account. He had toyed with the idea of returning all of the money to them but decided he was entitled to something out of it and settled for a commission, which he explained was payable to his colleague. He used the actual figure he received of £42,575 in the document and showed a fee of £1,825 as a deduction. The only explanation looking back now was mindless greed. Anyway, the Burtons were delighted and asked Tony to pop round to see them which he was reluctant to do, as he wanted to distance himself from them now. He did call on his way home from work, to be presented with an expensive case of wine, a voucher for £250 for Betty's Tea Rooms in Harrogate, and two chocolate lollies for the children. Mrs Burton was a little tearful when she handed the gifts over and said,

'It isn't much, Mr Needham, but we wanted to show our gratitude. We love to go to Betty's, and they do nice things for children as well.'

Something unusual happened to him at that moment. Maybe it was the unexpected nature of the gift, maybe there was something about Mrs Burton that reminded him of his mother, maybe it was the realisation of what he was doing, but his throat tightened, and his eyes moistened. For a second, he was unable to speak and leaned forward to kiss Mrs Burton on the cheek. He was surprised he did that as she had always been quite formal, but when he did, she put both of her arms around him and embraced him warmly. He was both touched and ashamed. He had gone so far down this road that he had managed until now to handle all situations almost without conscience, but this unexpected gesture, especially towards his children, had by-passed his normal defences. He apologised for his emotion, thanked her profusely, and was then on his way.

Jemma was delighted with the voucher, and the kids ate their chocolate lollies on the spot at the front door. The scene reminded Tony that his real prize was his family and the life they had together which he must now protect at all costs. He had closed most doors to the discovery of his criminal activities, and the last one was Stephanie. He was seeing Stephanie on the coming weekend, on a pre-planned break in Manchester. Tony had told Jemma that he was wrapping up his business dealings with his associates so that he could ready himself for the business he would eventually run with her father. So pleased was Jemma with that arrangement that she would almost have accepted anything that he wanted to do or any amount of time he wanted to stay away.

The weekend was, he decided, the last time he and

Stephanie would be together. The relationship had run its course, and he needed to end it, close down the last remnants of Baxter, and concentrate on his real business life back with the safety that went with legitimacy. On the Friday evening, he went home, showered, changed clothes, and packed a small bag. Jemma cooked for the kids and kissed him goodbye as he left the kitchen and the distracted children watching the TV.

'So, this is the last time you will be doing this then?' she asked, whilst smiling and stirring the food.

'I can't say that now, can I? Your dad might have me travelling all over the country making him and his pals rich.'

'No he won't, I won't let him.' She theatrically threw her head back in an assertive pose, and he thought about how much he loved her; how much he needed her. He looked at her for a few seconds, and she returned his look and said in a whispering voice, 'What?' He moved back into the room, kissed her on the lips and said,

'That's what. I love you so much.' With that, he was gone and driving to Manchester.

He arrived at the Radisson Blu Hotel, and the receptionist recognised him.

'Hello, Mr Baxter, how are you today?'

'Fine, thank you. I have a suite reserved.'

'Yes, of course, your wife has already checked in, but let me give you a separate key.' Tony took the key and the lift to the seventh floor. When he opened the door, Stephanie was sitting on the sofa dressed in the hotel robe and clearly nothing else. She had a glass of champagne in her hand and a bottle chilling in the silver bucket on the table.

'Oh, here is my husband after a hard day's work. I wonder how I can relax him.'

She poured him a drink and walked on her toes lightly towards him. She was warm, fragrant, and irresistible to him. He took the glass and sat with her on the sofa. Any thoughts of ending the relationship would have to wait, certainly until tomorrow. Tonight he would enjoy the setting, this sexy woman, and the last night of this part of his life. And he certainly did. All thoughts of home and stability were lost as Patrick Baxter took over and he became immersed in the second life he was leading.

The next morning he awoke with a heavy head, partly the champagne which kept flowing through the long night, but also the realisation that he had to break off this relationship. Every time he saw Stephanie he had a strong sexual attraction to her, but it was more than that. If he was Patrick Baxter, he would take her with him to whatever job he was going to. They would go everywhere together, for whatever time they stayed together, until the pleasure ran out. But he was not Patrick Baxter; he had a life, he had a wife, children, and a future, which could not involve her. He worried that his desire for her was still so strong and played for more time to enjoy being with her and to think. All day Saturday they behaved as they had done in London. They ate and drank when they felt like it in several places in Manchester, as well as returning to their hotel room like two teenagers using an empty parental home to indulge their sexual appetites. Tony expelled all thoughts of ending the relationship until the next day.

On Sunday morning they went downstairs into the dining room and ate breakfast quietly. Stephanie picked up the Financial Times and read for a few minutes whilst finishing her coffee, and they then returned to the room. She laughed as she produced the newspaper she had stolen from the dining room and popped into her handbag. She sat at their table and started to read it again. Tony sat opposite her at the table, looking at her and wondering right up until the moment he started speaking, if it was possible to keep the relationship. Was it possible to have the penny and the bun, this particular penny and this particular bun? The same old dilemmas played through his head about the deceit to Jemma and the kids, the dangers of a double life, and the risk of losing both. Yet here, sitting in front of him was a woman who excited him and found him very attractive, amongst all of the choices she must have. Ego had joined greed as cancers entering his system and confused him. Almost without thinking or knowing exactly what he was going to say, he started to speak.

'Stephanie, I have been offered a job abroad, and I am thinking of taking it.'

She looked up from her newspaper and took off the dark rimmed spectacles that were perched on the end of her nose, as she folded the paper and placed it on the table.

'Really? Where abroad?'

'Singapore.'

'Wow, that really is abroad. Who would you be working for?'

'Well, I say it is a job, but really it would be self-employment working as a consultant for one or two contacts

I have made.'

'Who are they then?'

'One of them is Carter Browne, who are looking to expand into the Far East, but don't say anything to anyone as it is very confidential.'

'So, what would you be doing for them?'

'Prospecting for contracts in Asia. They would pay me very generous expenses and then a percentage of the deals that I set up. It isn't just them; there are one or two others that I am speaking to.'

'So, would you be based there or just travel there regularly?'

'If I take the job I would have to live in Singapore, at least for a couple of years.'

'A couple of years? Ummm, well I get six weeks holiday a year, and I suppose I could throw the odd sicky.' A moment's silence as she looked at him and then her mood changed. 'Oh, hang on a minute, am I not being invited?'

'It's not that, Steph, it's just that it's not fair to you, and I really don't know what would be involved in accommodation, time frames, and stuff like that,' he answered, realising he was on a different path now and that he was likely to face an attack.

'What is this? Is this the brush off? Are you dumping me?'

The mood had upped to hostile, and Stephanie's eyes were wide open and displaying her outrage.

'No, no, I am just telling you what might happen and that we need to think about things and the practicalities that's all. I am trying to be honest with you, as I always have been.'

The irony of the last remark did not escape his attention as he fought to control the situation, but he ignored it as he continued his pitch. Midway through his next sentence, Stephanie stood up.

'I'm going for a shower,' she said coldly, as she marched into the bathroom.

'Come on, Steph; let's talk it through.'

'Fuck off,' she shouted, as she closed the bathroom door.

Tony heard the shower running and pondered the situation. He had played it badly, that was for sure, and his plan to ease gently out of the relationship was in tatters. He thought about repair and settled on telling her he would not take the job. He might even say he was worried he was falling in love with her and he had commitment issues. Yes, that was a good one, why hadn't he gone with that one. That would have played out much better, and he could have seen her a few more times and then written to her to say he just could not commit as he had failed in relationships before. He was formulating a plan and his opening gambit when he heard the bathroom door open on the other side into the generous dressing room of their suite.

'Stephanie, can we talk?' he shouted. There was no reply.

A few minutes later Stephanie appeared in her trouser suit carrying her handbag and walked purposefully towards the room door.

'Stephanie, please come and sit down,' he said gently,

but she opened the door and was gone without a word or a look back. Tony raced to the door, but she had marched to the lift which was opening for three people waiting on the seventh floor. One of the men stood to one side to let Stephanie enter as the lift doors opened and then they were gone.

Where had she gone, and would she be back? Tony quickly looked around the room. She had left her overnight bag, a sweater, some underwear, and some cosmetics. She had taken her toothbrush, perfume, and spare shoes. They must have been in the handbag, which was big enough, but why had she not taken the other stuff and her overnight bag? She must be coming back. Tony stayed around the hotel for the rest of the day and telephoned Stephanie's mobile regularly, but it always went to message. He ate in the room that night on his own and kept Baxter's phone beside him, even when ringing Jemma on his own phone. When talking to Jemma, he constantly stared at Baxter's lifeless mobile in front of him. He was due to go home today, but how could he in these circumstances? He needed to know if Stephanie was coming back. He rang Jemma and told her that something had come up, and he would have to stay one more night and come back tomorrow. She sighed but accepted the explanation.

'How are the kids, babe?' he enquired absently.

'Fine, but Anna has come out in spots today.'

'Spots? What kind of spots?' He suddenly tuned in.

'Not sure really, but it is like a rash.'

'RASH? Where is it?' he said, now fully engaged.

'It is mainly on her back and neck, but she seems to be ok, although a little tired.'

'Take her to the doctor, Jemma, or call the doctor out. It might be meningitis, and you can't take any risks with that.'

'It's not meningitis, Tony; she isn't running a fever.'

'Jemma, for God's sake, take her to the doctor and find out what it is. Don't take any risks.'

'All right, calm down. I will ring the surgery and ask the doctor to pop round just in case she is contagious. God, absent parent calling all the shots,' she said tartly.

'Do you want me to come home now?'

'No, not really, I am sure we can manage. Well, I always want you to come home of course, but you can finish your business deals, and I will sort this out. I almost wish I hadn't told you,' she said, her tone softening.

'I'm sorry, Jem, it's just that I do worry about them, especially illness, you know that.'

'Yes, I do. I will ring you once the doctor has been.'

A dark thought now entered his head. He was looking all of the time for an obvious trap or punishment for his deeds such as being found out, shamed, and losing his job or liberty. Perhaps God or the cosmos had a bigger punishment for him, like taking one of his children as a supreme punishment. The minutes started to pass as though in slow motion. No call from Stephanie, and no news from Jemma. He tried watching the television but was unable to concentrate on anything, just channel hopping and glancing at both phones. He drank the wine from the fridge in the room and then the gin and tonic, but nothing settled him until he dozed off to sleep lying on top of the bed. He dreamt that he walked into a field to try and find his car, but as he walked his feet become stuck in the mud. As quickly as he released one foot, the other became trapped. Eventually, he lay across the mud and crawled on his stomach, but then he could not see where he was going. He needed to find his car, but it was dark, and he couldn't find it. He heard his telephone ring from the car and tried to follow the noise, but became stuck again. The noise became louder until he awoke to find his phone ringing in front of him. It was Jemma.

'Hello,' he said, with a dry mouth.

'I thought you must have gone out when the phone kept ringing,'

'No, I must have nodded off, I haven't left the room. How is Anna?'

'It's chicken pox; the doctor has just left. She is fine. She has a bit of a temperature now, and we have to stop her scratching, but she will be off school for a couple of weeks.'

'Thank God for that.'

'It's alright for you because you will be at work. I will have to entertain her,' Jemma said with a laugh.

The relief was immense. The punishment of a dead child was not to be visited upon him, and he could relax. If only he knew what Stephanie was doing? He would wait tonight in the hope of her return. Did he need to worry?

Chapter 28

The night passed, and at 6.30 he woke up alone. He was wide awake, and now there was no doubt that Stephanie was not coming back to the hotel. He checked Baxter's phone, and there were no messages for him. He saw that he had telephoned Stephanie 17 times since she stormed out of the hotel. He lay in bed for another hour or so, trying to imagine what Stephanie was thinking and wondering if she was just the type of woman who walked off and you never heard from her again. Maybe she chalked it up to experience and would tell people that her last boyfriend was like all of the others, and she had moved on. Eventually, he decided to shower and get ready for breakfast, which he would have downstairs in the hope that she might decide to turn up and join him in a public place. He was surprisingly hungry and took a large English breakfast, which he ate heartily, but all of the time watching the entrance door just in case it was to be breakfast for two. It wasn't.

After he packed his things in the room, he picked up Stephanie's pink travel case and placed her sweater and underwear inside. He went into the bathroom and collected her toothpaste, cosmetics, and hairbrush. Hairbrush? Why would she leave that behind? A final check of the room and then he took the lift to reception where he saw the same receptionist who had checked him in.

'Hello, Gillian,' he said, glancing at her silver name badge.

'Good Morning, Mr Baxter, how are you today?'

'I'm fine, thanks. Mrs Baxter had to leave urgently last night, and I am in meetings all day today. I wonder if I can leave her bag with you so that she can collect it later.'

'Certainly, Mr Baxter, I will pass it to the concierge for safe keeping.'

Tony paid the bill, had a little chit chat with the very friendly Gillian, and walked to his car. Once inside, he checked Baxter's phone again and seeing nothing, sent a text to Stephanie. *'Good morning Stephanie. I seem to have upset you and worry that you misunderstood me. Can we talk? I have checked out of the hotel and left your case with the concierge. Please ring. Love Patrick xx'* He saw that his message was delivered and waited for a few minutes watching the screen for the little dots to show that a reply was being prepared, but there was nothing. Putting that phone away, he picked up his own, which was on silent, and saw that he had three missed calls, a message, and a text, all from Matthew Barker. The message asked him to ring as soon as he could, and the text dated yesterday read *'I know it is a weekend Tony, but I need to speak to you urgently. Can we meet today? Regards Matthew.'* Somehow, he had missed these messages with his panic about Anna. His instinct told him this was serious, but he couldn't imagine what it could be. He had tied up all loose ends, and there had not been any recent business dealings other than entirely legitimate ones. He telephoned Matthew and apologised for not ringing yesterday. Matthew breathlessly thanked him for ringing and asked where they could meet and said he didn't want to discuss it on the phone, but would rather tell him all about it face to face. He arranged to meet Matthew at lunchtime in a pub near the branch and drove home to change into his suit. It was an uncomfortable journey as the unpleasantness with Stephanie had both alarmed and upset him. He tried to think it may be a blessing in disguise as the relationship was surely over now, and he could concentrate on his domestic life, vowing to never cheat on Jemma again. What was on Matthew's mind that worried him so much he wanted a meeting on a weekend? Had he overlooked something? He ran through his checklist in his head and was sure he had covered everything.

He arrived home somewhat exhausted by the thought process, but he smiled and kissed Jemma at the door before visiting Anna in her room, who was glum and spotty.

'Can you stay with me today, Daddy, as I am so poorly?'

'No, I can't sweet pea, but I can take you out as soon as you are better and buy you an ice cream as big as your head. Shall we get raspberry ripple to match your face?' he said with a laugh and gave her a light tickle and a hug.

'Don't make me scratch, Daddy,' Anna said with a pained laugh and then hugged him deeply. Tony hugged her back and felt the wonderful warmth of a child's love. He wanted to stay and experience more of it, but he had things to do so he reluctantly pulled away.

Tony's morning was busy and varied and took his mind off his lunchtime meeting. There were new mortgage applications and two investment appointments, which helped the branch target and cemented his charmed life mood. He walked to the pub at lunchtime and saw Matthew, who was solemn looking, sitting in a quiet corner staring at what was left of a pint of Guinness. He was not wearing his normal ill-fitting suit, but an old pair of corduroy trousers and a grey woollen sweater. This did not look good and for that matter nor did Matthew.

'Hello, Matthew, you look like you have been out all night.' Matthew jumped up from his seat as though life had been injected back into him.

'Good of you to come, Tony. I am absolutely shitting myself.'

'What's the problem?'

'Well, it all stems from that infernal Burton family who have caused all hell to break out in the office. That new managing partner, Colin Ackroyd, hates my guts. I don't know, did I tell you about him? Anyway, he wants rid of me. He thinks I am a complete tosser and is looking for any excuse to push me out.'

'Just a minute, Matthew, I sorted the Burton matter out, and they were delighted. They even bought me a present. What can be the problem there?'

'It's their fucking daughter, Karen something or other. She has telephoned the office asking to see the file, and when my PA said she couldn't give her any information, she asked to speak to the senior partner and made a complaint to Ackroyd, the fucking cow.'

'Complaint? What sort of complaint?'

'Well, that's the point. She isn't the client, and my PA was right that she was not entitled to anything, but because she got through to Ackroyd she told him about you, and he said you didn't work for us and then it just all went down the toilet,' rambled Matthew.

At this point, Matthew started to cry noisily, and the two couples in the pub turned to look in his direction. The solicitor seemed to be disintegrating before Tony's eyes.

'Matthew, you are going to have to pull yourself together. How bad can it be?'

'How bad? How bad? I'll tell you how fucking bad. I'm suspended pending a full enquiry, and they want to have a look at all of my files over the last two years. They will want to talk to you about what you have done and who you have seen. They are going on about client confidentiality and work outside of our professional indemnity insurance because you were not an employee.'

Tony tried to remain calm for Matthew's sake, but his own heart was now pounding. Enquiries into all files, what did that mean? Would this be a forensic fine-tooth comb and a search into the recurring names of One Life and Patrick Baxter?

'Look, Matthew, every time I dealt with one of your clients I told them that I didn't work for the law firm and told them where I was from. Any information they were giving me was with full consent and in full knowledge of who I was. If any investment came to the building society, they knew about my background and had to go through our rules and regulations, which are at least as rigorous as yours.'

Matthew started to breathe a little easier, but he was still a gibbering wreck. He was a man of little confidence or ability, but with a high gloss polish provided by his background and education. That polish was peeling away and exposing a shallow man who believed he was about to lose everything, including the glue holding him together. He seemed to be calming, but added,

'Well, you might be right, Old Chap, but this Burton daughter has asked to see the documents relating to the sale of those bloody shares they lost. There is nothing on file about them at all, other than the enquiry they made when they realised they weren't there.'

Tony realised he hadn't told Matthew about the sale. He didn't do it deliberately but had never thought to tell him as he considered the matter complete when he returned the money, well, most of it. This really was a potential problem, but Tony was now not only experienced at dealing with the problems of his double life, but he had also developed a confidence bordering on arrogance at his own ability to escape. He was worried, but his calculating mind was already planning.

'Hang on, Matthew, I did trace the investment, but not the certificate. I arranged everything through Mrs Burton and got her money back for them, and she was delighted. That's why she bought me the present.'
Matthew thought for a second and then said,

'Well, that should be okay then. Can you give me all of the paperwork? I will complete the file and tell the odious Ackroyd that he can check it out himself.'

'That might be a problem as there was a confidentiality clause, and I'm not sure I kept a copy.'
Tony realised how weak that sounded, and even the

irredeemably naive Matthew looked at him dubiously.

'Well, surely the Burtons have a copy or the company can provide a duplicate,' he replied.

'Yes. Yes, I think you are right, and I may even have one myself back at the office. Let me check that before you go back to Ackroyd.'

Matthew was too wound up in his own problems to make further enquiries himself, but Tony realised the seriousness of the position and how thin his explanation sounded. He cursed himself again for his greed in taking some of the money as a commission, which would make it more difficult to explain. He could have just changed the dates on copies of the original deed, and any enquiry would find that the full payout had gone to the owner, but now if he did that there would be bound to be an enquiry as to who the middle man was who received the commission. That directly tied him to his alias of Baxter. He almost coloured with anger at himself for mindless greed over such a small amount of money in the circumstances.

He spent the next half an hour soothing Matthew's nerves and ensuring that he would not speak to anybody but him over these matters until they could conclude them satisfactorily. They said their goodbyes, and Tony returned to his office. During the afternoon appointments he went through the now-familiar process of speaking to customers and dealing with their requests, but in the background, he was playing out his own situation and trying to find a solution. By the time the 4.30 appointment left he felt he had a plan. He would go and see Mrs Burton and persuade her that her daughter was causing him a problem and that he should not have tried to help. He would say it was now causing a problem at the firm of solicitors because of Karen. He felt confident that Mrs Burton would feel guilty and be susceptible to his suggestion to ring Ackroyd to say there was no complaint as well as telling Karen to keep out of it. He was confident that the very decent Mrs Burton would be embarrassed by her daughter causing an issue. She might even be persuaded to tell Ackroyd to stop asking for documentation. Yes, that was it. Mrs Burton was the key here, and he felt there was a lot of goodwill there. Ackroyd was a problem, especially if he was going to look at all the files, but let's sort out Burton first and then deal with others if they come up. He allowed himself to review recent events. He thought about how good he had been at problem-solving, controlling those in contact with him, and building his escape route. That route was now in sight. He would be able to access the money, live his family life, and get away with his crimes. These were just loose ends, and he had the skill to tie them up. He once again pictured the plate spinning act and had a clear vision of the end of the act and the orderly collection of the spinning plates.

He was feeling a little smug about what seemed such a clever and complete plan when Theresa Mullin leaned through the door into his office.

'Just off home now, Tony. You are the last one tonight.'

'Thanks, Theresa, I'll set the alarm. I just have a couple of things to do before I go. Goodnight.'

Theresa returned his goodnight and moved away before remembering something and pushing the door open again.

'Oh did Maureen get hold of you this afternoon?'

'No, I have had appointments all afternoon. Why?'

'There was a woman in at lunchtime asking to see someone she said worked here and she was a little insistent even when Maureen said we didn't have anyone by that name.'

'Who was she asking for,' Tony asked, as he rose from his desk.

'Patrick Baxter.'

Chapter 29

Even the unflappable Tony Needham couldn't hide his shock at the news of an enquiry about Patrick Baxter at the branch. Only Georgina Pilkington and her friend Mandy knew of any connection between the two, but both of them knew that Baxter did not work in that office. Theresa could not help with a description of the woman as she had not seen her and Maureen had not given any details. Who could it be? Maureen could not have been too alarmed as he did have gaps between his appointments and if she was really worried, surely she would have interrupted him. What sort of enquiry had the woman made? The word insistent was used. That was a worry in that it implied the woman expected Baxter to be there. Could it be Mrs Burton's daughter Karen who was already causing problems? No it couldn't, because neither she nor her parents were aware of Patrick Baxter. Unless she had told the police and they had traced the transaction on the Midland Bank investment and had found Baxter's account. Surely not.

Tony sat for a few more minutes trying to solve the puzzle. He had been so very careful and there were no leads back to him from any of his dealings. Had someone used a private detective to trace steps? Why would they? Who would do that and what did they want. Was it Dominic Price whose pride had been dented in the negotiation? And if it was, what could he now want, as exposure would be catastrophic for Price's business too. Whoever it was, this was bad. He tried to find that controlling side to his personality that had solved all problems so far. They just seemed to be popping up all over, despite his ability to solve them. The plates were in danger of falling.

Having set the alarm, Tony walked to his car with his head spinning. He sat in the car and looked at himself in the vanity mirror to see a worried man looking back, a man who appeared to have aged. He started the car and drove to his home, pulling up on the drive and taking a deep sigh, but so relieved to be back to his place of safety. As the headlamps illuminating the front door dimmed, he saw Jemma at the front bay window smiling at him and then Anna joined her and waved furiously as to indicate her health was improving. Toby then joined in and jumped up and down at the window around his mother and sister, pretending to be an ape. Tony laughed at this blissful domestic scene and the well lit living room warmth that was the background to this idyllic family picture. He took a moment or two to take in this normal family scene and absorb the warmth from it to calm him down. There in that picture were the most important aspects of his life, so clear now as he gazed at them. He would soon close that front door and be safe from the constant thinking that was draining him so much.

Raising her hand to signal him to get a move on, Jemma was joined by the two children imitating her. Jemma's hand then lowered slowly as her attention was taken by something behind Tony's car. The smile on her face fell away, an expression of bemusement replacing it. Anna also looked at something as Toby stared at his mother and her change of mood. Tony looked in his rear view mirror, but could not see anything so he opened the car door, got out and saw a figure standing in the drive glaring at his family. It was Stephanie.

"You complete fucking bastard," she said without blinking or moving. Tony turned to look at his family who were now staring back in a confused, concerned way. This woman on their driveway was clearly not lost and seeking directions, nor a friend of the family. Although they could not hear her, they could see in her manner and demeanour that her approach was aggressive.

"Stephanie… I can explain," was all he could manage in a panic stricken voice.

"I bet you can you shit, why don't we go in and you can explain it to your family?" again delivered unblinking. All he could think was to escape and remove Stephanie from the driveway. He opened the passenger door and tried to push her in, but she resisted. Jemma's expression had now turned to real alarm as Tony ran around to the driver's side and jumped in, leaning over to the still open passenger door.

"Please Stephanie get in and we can talk. PLEASE." To his immense immediate relief she did get in and Tony reversed quickly, threw the car into forward gear and sped off out of the street.

"It isn't what you think Stephanie, really it isn't."

"It isn't what I think? Patrick Baxter is not your real name, you are married with kids and you have lied to me from the moment you met me… IT'S NOT WHAT I

FUCKING THINK?" she screamed the last sentence which was delivered with such ferocity that Tony momentarily took his eyes from the road and had to swerve to miss a parked car.

"I wanted to tell you and nearly did a few times, but I just couldn't."

"Tell me what? Your real name, what you do for a living, who you are still married to?"

"No it's not like that. Just calm down and we will go somewhere where we can talk and I will tell you everything."

Although Stephanie had not agreed, she had at least calmed down and began to cry.

"I just can't believe that I have been so stupid and been taken in by a con man that I let into my heart. To think that I have fallen for all that shit you have been feeding me." Tony saw up ahead a Premier Inn sign and pulled into the car park.

"Will you come in here with me and let me explain," he said as he fought to control the situation. If he could get her somewhere private he could try and figure a way out. She seemed prepared to do it. They wordlessly walked in to the hotel, but there was only a small bar and there were already a few people there.

"A room please," Tony requested to his surprise. Stephanie stood silently behind him with her mascara staining her cheeks from her tears and the receptionist looking at her knowingly.

"Double or single?" the receptionist asked without

expression.

"Double please."

"Will that be just for one night?" was the uncomfortable next question.

"Yes, just one night thank you."

"Will you want an early morning call or a newspaper?"

"No thank you, just the room."

Tony realised that he did not have any Baxter credit or debit cards and in the absence of cash had to use his Needham card. He had no alternative, other than to leave and the chances of getting Stephanie back in the car were not good. He used the card and in any event the cat was out of the bag with Stephanie.

They walked the two flights of stairs into room 207. The room was sparse, but comfortable with a double bed, table, two chairs and a heavy glass bowl on the table.

"Not quite what we are used to Stephanie," he said with a smile as an ill timed light remark.

"Fuck off Patrick or is it Tony?" was the terse response.

"Sorry Stephanie, sorry for everything. Can we sit down? When did you find out?"

"I waited in my car outside the hotel and followed you back here to see where you went. I saw you go into your house and your office and saw what a complete shit you are." she answered with real venom. He had no idea what he was going to say or do. He was now flying on adrenalin alone and saw no clear pathway. His instinct was to calm the woman in front of him and come up with some explanation that might win him time or even save him.

His mind was empty and maybe for that reason he told the truth.

"My name is Tony Needham. I am married to Jemma and I have two children. As you seem to have worked out, I am a manager of a building society in Harrogate and I have got myself involved in something that meant I invented Patrick Baxter. I never imagined that all of this would happen, but once I started I couldn't stop. If I could go back in time I would undo a lot of what I have done and maybe appreciate what I had in my life. I never set out to have an affair, but when I saw you it just happened and I couldn't control my attraction to you. If I have hurt you, then I am truly sorry and it may be that it will have cost me my marriage and possibly even more than that."

As he said the last part, a genuine single tear squeezed out of his right eye and slowly edged its way down his cheek before he brushed it away. Stephanie watched it fall, but showed no emotion or gave any response to it. Tony continued.

"If it is any consolation, I have never felt as lonely as I feel now or as afraid. I know I don't deserve to feel any better and there is nothing you can say that will make me feel any worse than I already feel. I don't know what to do or what you want to do."

Stephanie continued to stare but said, "I wanted to hear the truth and to know what you were really all about. I warned you not to mess me about, but you did anyway."

"Do you want me to leave Jemma and the kids and live with you?" he asked, not entirely sure why but perhaps testing if he had an escape route.

"What makes you think I could live with a lying pig

like you?" she spat back.

"Well what do you want?"

"I wanted to know who you were and what your game has been, so that I maybe can avoid people like you in the future. Maybe it's me. Maybe I just get attracted to the wrong people."

"It's not you Stephanie, really it isn't. I was in the middle of something… something to do with business and it all got carried away with itself. I never intended to hurt anybody, I never meant to lose myself, but that is what I did."

The last thought summed up how he felt at that moment, discovered as a fraud in every way and ashamed of the lies and deceit, but the feeling was quickly replaced by fear, fear of consequences and a desperate desire to save himself and salvage the situation, or as much of it as he could.

"You see Stephanie the reason I pulled away was that I could feel myself falling in love with you and I had gone too far with this Patrick Baxter thing. I nearly told you the truth many times, but I just couldn't find the words. I wanted to pull away from you but every time I did, I was pulled back towards you. I am so so sorry for everything." Stephanie seemed to be softening as she pulled out a handkerchief from her bag to dry her tears without taking her eyes off him. She sighed and leaned back in the chair which signalled to Tony that she was more under control now.

"I know I have hurt you Stephanie and would like to make it up to you in some way. Is there any way?" He really had no idea where this was going or what Stephanie might now want. She had apparently calmed herself, but was not responding. He blundered on after a few seconds of silence. "Would you let me buy you a flat… or, or us a flat so that we can still see each other or you just have the flat and you don't need to see me at all. Anything that you want… anything that might make up for all of this."

Stephanie got up from her seat and walked to the mirror on the wall to straighten her hair. Tony looked to the floor in the hope that he had started dialogue that would lead to some sort of peaceful agreement. Perhaps the money would come in handy after all. It was because he was distracted by this sudden optimism, his now track record of wriggling out of danger and using his charm to full capacity that he didn't notice Stephanie turn from the mirror to pick up the heavy glass bowl. He didn't see anything, just felt a heavy blow to the right side of his head which did not immediately cause pain. It felt like someone had switched off the lights and emptied his head of all thoughts. There were black spots in each eye that swirled like black snow in his vision as he fell to his knees on the floor. The pain had just registered when he turned from his kneeling position as Stephanie screamed and brought the bowl down on him again. This time he moved to avoid the full impact, but the bowl struck his left cheek, just under his eye and opened a gash from which warm bright red blood covered his face. He could feel the dampness on his collar from the blood as he watched the deflected bowl leave Stephanie's hand and smash against the wall.

Stephanie jumped at him scratching and screaming as he tried to get up. They tangled arms and legs, until Tony gained some grip to cause them to fall onto the bed. Tony managed to pin her flailing arms and legs by lying on top of her and trapping her legs between his, as well as using his torso to hold down her right arm. He grabbed her left arm with his right hand and tried to quieten her shouts by putting his left hand over her mouth. Her eyes were wide open with vivid red veins in them, bright against the expanse of whiteness. The hand over her mouth had stopped the screaming, but the muffled noise was still loud. The noise must be bringing people to the room he realised, but with surprising strength she wriggled free of his hold and in an attempt to regain control they both fell heavily onto the floor with a sickening thud. Tony lost consciousness at that moment.

Chapter 30

He did not know how long he was unconscious. It could have been seconds or minutes. He had no memory of a dream during that time, just blackness and emptiness. He was woken by a banging on the room door and somebody shouting.

'Is everyone alright in there? Open this door; open this door.'

His mouth was dry, and his head was sore, very sore, as he slowly roused himself. He was lying on the floor with his right leg bent up against the bed. Stephanie was lying below him, and his left hand was still on her mouth. He pulled away, and her mouth remained slightly open, as were her lifeless eyes. He lifted himself to his feet and looked helplessly as the banging on the door continued. Was she dead? How had she died? She certainly looked dead as those blank staring eyes looked at the ceiling. Her head was at an angle to her body. Was her neck broken in the fall? Did his hand stay over her mouth when they were unconscious? The banging became louder, and the voice threatened,

'Open this door, or I am calling the police.'
Tony grabbed his jacket and his car keys before opening the door and brushing past three people in the corridor. There was no plan, no thought, just an instinct to run.

The sight of him and the circumstances stopped any of the people at the door interfering with him, but he heard a scream from one of them as she entered the room. Tony was already down the first flight of stairs by then and soon in his car. His hands were shaking so hard that he couldn't manage to get the ignition key in the lock for the first few attempts. Eventually, he did and started the car, almost reversed into a van, and drove off into the night. He wasn't going anywhere in particular, just driving anywhere. He found himself on a village road and drove up a deserted track to sit and think. His body was now shaking uncontrollably as his telephone continued to bleep messages. He began to sob in the utter desolation that now engulfed him, as the realisation of the loss of everything seemed to invade every sinew of his body. There comes a time with real sobbing that the body can sob no more. It is almost as though all of the tears have been spent and the shaking and tremors of the body are exhausted. He could not be sure when that happened, but at some point, he fell into a deep sleep.

When he woke, it was just after 5 am and he had nowhere to go. He sat staring out of the window for what appeared to be an eternity as all of his energy had left him. Summoning up some strength, he started the car and drove, without thinking, back to Harrogate which had an eerie quiet as the town began to prepare for the day. There were some delivery vans driving around, and the bakery was opening up as he pulled into his normal parking spot at the back of the society building. Nobody saw him enter the code to gain access to the office or paid any attention to the lights going on. He poured himself a glass of water and sat in his chair after closing his door. He had run out of possibilities and hope. He had been seen, his credit card used, and the trace was going to be back to him. He had been so close to a complete plan, a life with his family, and those extra things that had seemed so important at one time. Those extra things that would now rob him of everything he once had. He would start his recollection of how he had reached this stage.

It was now 9am, and he could hear more voices in the branch. Hard to believe that the last ten minutes of review had taken him up to yesterday… yesterday. Yesterday morning he was living his life with a future, a wife who loved him, children who adored him, and a glittering career ahead of him. Was it so bad that he wanted a little more? He had gambled everything he had to get that little bit more and lost. It was the third knock on the door that he heard, but in any event, Melanie Forrester had decided to come in, as she did not hear a reply. As she opened the door, she saw her boss sitting in his leather chair just looking at her. His hair was matted with blood, his cheek wearing a crimson slash, and below a dishevelled jacket was a ripped and bloodstained shirt.

'Oh My God, Tony, what on earth has happened to you? Do you need to go to the hospital?'

'No, Melanie, I will be fine. What can I do for you?' he answered in his usual calm voice.

'There are two policemen here wanting to talk to you, Tony,' she said, still shocked.

'Send them in, Melanie; send them in.'

If you enjoyed A Tangled Web, you'll love Simmering Rage, the new novel by John McArdle.

When you get into your car and drive anywhere, you take a gamble. You know that you should concentrate and drive carefully for all of the reasons that are very familiar. The thing over which you have no control is who you will encounter, how they will behave, and what might happen to you.

Andy Connolly is a businessman who is recovering from his divorce, coming to terms with the expense of running two houses, and simply going home after a day at work.

However, a traumatic event on the drive home puts him in contact with a very dangerous man and the meeting changes his life forever. He is drawn unwillingly into a world that is foreign to him, filled with danger and from which he cannot escape.

Andy's closet ally is his sister Laura, who tries to help but is fighting her own demons and hiding a secret from her brother and the rest of the world. How will she deal with her brother's problems whilst trying to hide her own? How will she protect her child from danger she could not have predicted?

This clash of the criminal world and the ordinary person is filled with tense uncertainty. Who to trust? The police? The senior police officer is a man driven by ambition… and possibly other motives.

How can a life hang so drastically on a chance encounter? How can innocent people become targets simply through association?

Next time you get in your car just hope that you not only stay in your correct lane but in the world that is familiar to you.

The spell binding new novel by John McArdle is due out in June 2019. Contact info@jjmoffs.co.uk and order your first edition copy, signed by the author, and sent to you prior to release.